OPERATION A-MEN

HENRI YIRE

AMVPS

Published by

AMV Publishing

P.O. Box 661
Princeton, NJ 08542-0661
Tel: 609-785-5135 Fax: 609-7164770
emails: publisher@amvpublishingservices.com &
customerservice@amvpublishingservices.com
worldwide web.amvpublishingservices.com

Operation A-Men

Book & Cover Design: AMV Origination & Design Division

Library of Congress Control Number: 2013918758

ISBN: 978-0-9894917-0-9 (PB)

This is a work of fiction. Names, characters, businesses, places, events and incidents are either the products of the author's imagination or used in a fictitious manner. Any resemblance to actual persons, living or dead, or actual events is purely coincidental

To the conveyor of true knowledge who gave me access
to a hidden conspiracy

"If a nation expects to be ignorant and free, in a state of civilization, it expects what never was and what never will be."

— *Thomas Jefferson.*

"…in a Nation where they will not be judged by the colour of their skin but by the content of their character."

— *Martin Luther King Jr.*

ACKNOWLEDGEMENTS

My profound gratitude goes to Racheal Dennison, Jennifer Nlewedim and Victor Macford who contributed immensely in "testing" the validity of the plots and the believability of the characters. Chibudo Ahukanna, my biggest believer (fan doesn't exactly sum it all up) and book addict extraordinaire, David Motutu, my literary accomplice and enthusiast who like me is a true believer in conspiracies.

To Ronke Macauley of ANGELWORKS (my PR) who inspired me to see the world from a writer's perspective and opened me up to the many-sided and charismatically convoluted "business" of writing.

PROLOGUE

ERNEST ARCHIBONG HAD ALWAYS PRIDED HIMSELF on being a very observant person so it did not take him long to spot the kid. It was the second time he was coming to the church that day. The first time, he had just walked in speaking to nobody, knelt before the altar and after about fifteen minutes got up abruptly and left.

It was a very strange thing for a lad that young to do. He couldn't be more than ten years old.

Working in a church for years had given Ernest the perceptive abilities of a wizened owl and the rare opportunity to have seen all sorts. He adjusted his security uniform thoughtfully as he once more regarded the boy from his vantage position on the top floor balcony.

Why wasn't the lad in school or running around like any other normal kid?

Ernest waited for him to finish, then walked all the way to the entrance, past the pews etched with the names of loyal church contributors both dead and alive and positioned himself at the entrance.

The lad started forward; he had lost the spring in his step. His shoulders were hunched awkwardly and he was bent forward like he was carrying something heavy on his back.

He stopped in front of Ernest who was blocking the aesthetically arched church entrance but did not look up. With his head still bowed, he began pulling at his fingers twiddling a few of them nervously. Ernest slowly put one hand on the boy's shoulder and with the other lifted his face.

He was completely taken aback.

It wasn't the tears that shocked him. The lad was obviously sad but there was a glow on his face that was at a complete contrast to the tears.

Several words rushed to Ernest's mind trying to describe the expression on the boys face but only one made sense.

The look on the lad's face could only be described as divine.

⌘ ⌘

Fifteen minutes later the lad had calmed down enough to be able to give his name as Femi Adele. Sitting straight up in Ernest's small office clutching a bottle of coke which he just stared at without drinking, he began to stutter through his story. What he relayed to Ernest provoked an unexpected ill digestion problem for him.

He stared speechless at the boy. *How could a lad that young grasp such a vision and relay it with such eerie clarity that was both bone-chilling and detailed to the letter?*

⌘ ⌘

There was a shepherd in the mountains that owned a hundred sheep. He would put the sheep to pasture daily and controlled them by pointing out to them, with a crooked staff, the area to graze on. He was well stricken in age but handled his staff with much strength and precision. One day after putting the sheep to pasture he suddenly, without warning, stopped in his tracks, dropped the staff and began to claw at his throat, gasping for air. He looked around, desperately seeking help but all he had around him were his sheep and the foreboding shape of the mountains that surrounded them.

He dropped to his knees as the choking persisted; clawed

his clothes off his body throwing it aside. All the sheep, as if at a signal, stopped grazing and stared at the choking shepherd; unable to help.

The shepherd dropped stiffly to the ground, thrashed some more and eventually lay still, his lifeless form adding a touch of grey to the otherwise bright horizon.

Almost immediately, vultures began to circle and swoop slowly down. Within minutes, they had gathered around the corpse, helping themselves to the unexpected offering, roughly picking flesh from the bones of the once vibrant shepherd.

After the vultures had gone, the sheep began to move to different directions, every sheep going his own way. They began to scatter.

One sheep happened to stumble on the shepherds discarded staff and cloak and muzzled at it rolling it over.

A strange thing began to happen.

The sheep that had muzzled the cloak and staff suddenly rose up on its hind legs and stood upright like a man. It quickly put on the dead shepherd's cloak and brandished his staff. Looking around, it raised the shepherd's crooked staff and pointed it at the departing animals. Almost immediately the scattering sheep began to slowly converge, assembling as before. As if nothing had happened, the sheep returned to their grazing.

All the while, the transformed sheep had its head bowed with the cloak's hood covering its face. Finally, it shook it off and looked up.

A while ago, it had been a sheep but without warning had suddenly transformed into something else.

A man.

Another shepherd.

CHAPTER 1

TBS, Lagos. 9.05 a.m.

IT WAS THE WEEKEND. THE POLO CLUB AT TAFAWA Balewa Square was teeming with pressmen. There was an important game in the offing and the venue, with a capacity of three thousand spectators, was packed full. Government delegates were arriving to watch the game in the place of their invited superiors. There was a political attachment to almost every corporate function in Nigeria. If you were opportuned to be invited to one, your refusal could possibly mean a no confidence vote for you in the nearest future. If you could not make the function, a delegate was the next and most reasonable option. The representative of the Minister of Youth and Sports was already comfortably seated in the VIP section.

A huge white stable truck with an impressive insignia of a polo player arrived and word went round that Senator Amos Akintade was around. Senator Amos was an ardent lover of the game of polo and had been for almost fifteen years of his life. He had recently become a part-owner of the renowned Polo Club in Lagos after investing a sizeable income when the call for its privatization had been made by the incumbent governor. He was to be a major feature in the day's game and had made sure that everybody that was anybody would turn up. The pressmen in a flurry of activity surrounded the truck and cameras began flashing.

A small red Golf car had arrived some ten minutes ago and was parked discreetly a few yards from the Polo Club. At the backseat of the car, cradled carefully so as not to roll about were five new polo sticks otherwise known as mallets.

The man in the car whistled softly as he studied the layout of the club. He hurriedly took off his jacket and underneath it was the official vest for staffers of the Polo Club. Gingerly arranging his staff I.D. round his neck, he stepped out of the car.

⌘ ⌘

Senator Akintade was glowing with pride. He studied the crowd in attendance and grinned.

The whole city has come out to see me play.

If any man had a knack for manipulating the media for their personal good, the Senator was top on the list. The press invitations had been personally supervised and sent out by him. Balding with a spatter of white hair amongst the surviving strands, a team of worry lines on his forehead and a nose meant for a larger face, he looked like a senator should — serious and severe. He had been blatantly tagged in the last edition of the famed *Ovation* magazine as the "media spinner of the year". A well-deserved title as he had with an ingenious approach quelled the uproar that ensued after one of the chieftains of his political party was accused of shacking up with a minor. The fiasco involving the minor had quickly disappeared from the headlines amidst the rubble of, in the Senator's words, "more pressing and credible dispositions".

It had only taken a few calls.

Cameras flashed insistently as pressmen scuttled after the Senator trying to get the best shot- angle. They were all over him and it was all his oversized secret service details could do to create a path for him to pass through.

"Senator, does the polo game today have any connection to the upcoming elections in your zone?"

"Are your wife and kids in attendance today?"

A zealous pressman did a spectacular lunging and rudely cut across the Senator's path. One of the security service details grabbed him, roughly shoving him aside. The pressman stumbled and fell to the floor. The Senator stopped and turning to the security detail conjured up a frown.

"Greg, that was naughty of you. These people are my guests you know?"

"Eh... I'm sorry Sir."

The Senator stooped and in a dramatic pose, slowly picked up the fallen pressman. The media went to work catching the gesture on film. It was sure to make the headlines the next day.

"Senator, please smile for the cameras."

The smile was disarming.

⌘ ⌘

The contractors wanted the kill to be a spectacular one. They had requested for the whole works to be thrown in and wanted the press involved. It was strange for a hit to require media presence but since they were paying well they were entitled to the entertainment. Egunu never backed down on any demand.

He had given the contract adequate thought over the weeks. What they wanted was a blend of spectacle and publicity excluding any foul play. It had to be an accident until a thorough autopsy was conducted. No guns or weapon of any kind could be involved. The idea finally came when he read an article about the Senator's love of polo and the Polo Club in which he played actively. Five minutes later, he was on the phone putting through an international call to Ghana.

The stakeout of the Polo Club had taken several weeks. Every detail had to be critically analyzed. The plan had to be watertight. A crooked employee had parted with the staff paraphernalia for a modest sum and another one had allowed Egunu a one-hour tour of the polo pitch for, as he was told, "a magazine feature". Pictures and films of the Senator's past polo games had been easily gotten from the websites of local newspapers.

It was starting. The band began to play the Nigerian National Anthem as everybody stood at attention. Outside, staff of the Polo Club began unpacking the equipment in Senator Akintade's truck.

Egunu mixed in with them. No one noticed the new comer.

⌘ ⌘

"But Amos, tomorrow is Sunday, the kids have to attend Sunday school," intoned Bunmi Akintade, staring fixedly at her husband.

Senator Amos reared up slowly in anger. A wounded bull would have made a better sight.

"When I say something in this house Bunmi, it is not debatable. You hear me?"

"But they need…"

"Don't but me woman! The kids are to be at home in the morning tomorrow to watch the opening of the polo tournament. I am playing, so I expect my kids to watch their father and not some dammed clergyman in some God forsaken church!"

"Amos!"

She whirled around in anger and marched out of the room. He chuckled softly at her dramatic exit then called after her sweetly.

"Woman, before you start sulking, get me my cup of tea, okay?"

As an afterthought, he added. "Sugar please, no honey."

He smiled wickedly and started humming a tune under his breath.

⌘ ⌘

Unnoticed, Egunu switched the bag of mallets in the Senator's truck with the one he was carrying. They were identical copies.

⌘ ⌘

The two opposing teams were lined up facing each other as they waited for the umpire to throw the ball signaling the start of the first chukker. The air was tense with expectation as over three thousand spectators sat glued to the game. The pure thorough breed ponies neighed impatiently as they tried to hurry the game along. The umpire nodded and put the whistle to his lips.

⌘ ⌘

Egunu was sitting across the table listening to the aged Ghanaian speak. On the table between them lay five polo mallets. The Ghanaian blinked his small eyes continuously as he spoke. He was an imp of a man with a bushy entourage of mustache that adorned only his upper lip and ears that stuck out at right angles.

He has the look of a chimpanzee and the brain of a genius.

"The principle is quite simple, but the idea is simply ingenious!" the Ghanaian explained excitedly in his soft-spoken manner, smiling for effect.

The man known simply as "Baba M" had once in the prime of his life been hand picked along with several others by the

Ghanaian government to participate in a nuclear research engineering project that was high profile and top secret. He had worked for the state for years coming out with such startling discoveries in science that was inspiring. The catch came when in a research on certain radioactive elements he was exposed to a dangerously high amount of radioactivity. He passed out and had to remain in the hospital for months.

He was never the same again.

He began experiencing what the doctors called traumatic shock spells which would leave him shivering and sweating for hours and at such times an alarming rate of amnesia would assail him. He became a nervous wreck. The research institute had finally pulled him out, giving him an award for exemplary governmental service despite his adamant protest that he was okay. He wrote several letters to the institute to demand a reinstatement but none of his letters were ever replied.

"They hand me cheques every month and expect me to be content, they won't even allow me into my lab for as much as a remembrance tour". He often complained to anyone who cared to listen to his incessant ramblings.

He was like a child seeking a lollipop. Anything that allowed him into the world of science was enough incentive for him. The assassin became his frequent customer.

Egunu cleared his throat loudly bringing the man in front of him back to the present.

"Baba M, how does it work?"

⌘ ⌘

The game had begun.

The riders and their 900 pound pure or thoroughbred ponies galloped down the field. An offside stroke from one of the players sent the ball flying to the center of the field. The crowd came alive cheering.

⌘ ⌘

Baba M began the inevitable science lecture.

"A tiny electron charged ball is triggered and travels through the length of the slender graphite body of the mallet and into an electromagnetic field in the metallic handle. The resonance it creates is magnified a thousand times in the electric field and the cadmium/nickel charged metallic ball releases an electric charge which is converted into a thousand volts of live electricity. The person holding the mallet at that moment is exposed to a high degree of electrical shock. A man could go through a few hundred volts of electricity and come out unscathed, maybe with only a dizzy spell and a persistent headache but a thousand volts of electricity would instantly kill any man. The effect after five minutes would completely disappear; cause of death unknown."

The assassin nodded slowly, raised an eyebrow and asked.

"What sets the whole process off, and when is it triggered?"

Baba M blinked, looking a bit flustered.

"Didn't I tell you? I'm so sorry charle'. It must have skipped my mind," he smiled apologetically.

"Well, when the mallet hits the polo ball with considerable force, the little beauty goes off instantly."

It was only then that Egunu relaxed and smiled.

⌘ ⌘

"Mummy, I don't want to watch the polo games."

"Bade, your father insists that you kids watch him play today."

"But mummy, today's Sunday school and..."

"No complaints children, you have to respect your father's wishes," she intoned gravely.

Senator Akintade's children still grumbling their disapproval sat down to watch the polo games being broadcasted live on TV.

⌘ ⌘

The Senator galloped after a free ball. He was like a knight swooping down on the enemy. He lifted the mallet in a smooth arc and swung it towards the ball. The roar of the crowd was deafening.

⌘ ⌘

Near the entrance of the club the staffers were huddled together watching the game. The assassin sitting amongst them was only interested in one rider. He zoomed in on Senator Akintade's charge with his binoculars and waited expectantly. *The predator was coming in for the kill.*

⌘ ⌘

By a tremendous foresight, the Senator abruptly halted in his charge for the ball and swerving unexpectedly to the right avoided an opponent's attempt at hooking his mallet to spoil his shot. The pony anticipating his rider's move by a combination of constant practice and pure polo sense, obeyed the Senator's move to the letter. The opponent unable to stop on time charged past the Senator creating an open path to the goal. The Senator stooped and urged the pony on. He lifted the mallet again. The crowd became uncontrollable.

Egunu zoomed in catching the Senator in his sights.

⌘ ⌘

"..Eh..., what did you say?" Senator Akintade's wife was shouting above the sound of the blender in the kitchen.

"Mummy I said that daddy is going to score!" The children where frantic with excitement.

"I know, just try to keep the volume of the TV down, you hear?"

They weren't listening.

⌘ ⌘

It was like magic.

The crowd fell silent. Everyone stared at Senator Akintade's thrashing figure on the ground. It was the press that recovered first. They burst past security and unto the field. Flashbulbs began to go off.

At the entrance, Egunu lowered his binoculars, adjusted his glasses, and slowly left the Polo Club in the confusion that ensued.

⌘ ⌘

"Mummy! Mummy! Daddy is injured, come and see."

"What did you say?" she hollered back.

"I said daddy is injured!"

"You'll have to speak louder. I can't hear a word of what you're saying."

⌘ ⌘

The crowd was alive again but this time with hushed murmurings. The security men went to work barring the press who were more interested in taking a shot of the fallen man than in helping him recover. Medical examiners were allowed through and the body was finally stretchered off the field. In the privacy of the medical center of the Polo Club, away from the noise and people, the chief medical examiner looked over the body and scowled.

"I don't believe it… he… he's dead," he declared to no one in particular.

The medical examiner straightened and shook his head in confusion.

"The man was as fit as a fiddle. I personally gave him a check up last week."

⌘ ⌘

The Golf car left the polo club unnoticed. At the back lying unused were the real mallets belonging to the late Senator. Egunu dialled a number on his cell phone and slowed at the traffic light as the connection was made.

"The contract has been executed accurately. Confirmation will be received in this evening's news. The balance of the money should be in the account by morning."

A voice at the other end asked. "Did everything go as arranged?"

There was a long silence then the assassin said softly. "Judgment was pronounced as deserved."

"We have something new for you."

The line went dead.

CHAPTER 2

TO OBTAIN EVEN THE SMALLEST AMOUNT OF radioactive phosphate from the deposit at Ogun State you had to go through a rigid routine of endorsement from the authorities involved and even with that it would take at least a month before you could as much as see it, and an extra week for its delivery to be effected. The fact that this procedure had been strictly adhered to for years without any form of alteration, coupled with the knowledge that the order allegedly came straight from the Speaker of the National Assembly further baffled him. *Why would a prominent member of the National Assembly issue an order for radioactive phosphate to be delivered to a warehouse in Lagos State?*

The interesting aspect to it all was that the order was to be delivered in one week.

One week!

Tade Joseph did not like the development one bit. As Head of Science Procurement and Delivery, he was a suspicious fellow by nature and a stickler to the rules. He had fortified his career climb by careful hard work and sticking to the books. Petite and balding at thirty-six with more than a casual love for the art of drinking, he sensed something suspicious was going on. He owed it to his conscience to at least verify the authenticity of the claim. Radioactive phosphate is not just any kind of chemical substance. It is rated a "type A" regenerator. Handled incorrectly it can be quite lethal, boiling a man's insides in minutes.

Who can I talk to about this?

There was one man who would definitely know. He picked up his phone and dialed a number.

"Science Research Institute, good morning," the voice at the other end said, mechanically.

"Good morning, my name is Tade Joseph and I would like to speak with Mr. Onome Agoro please."

"Hold on while I get him please." He drummed his fingers on the table as he waited. The line came alive.

"Hello?"

"Hello Onome, its Tade. I need a favor."

"Hello my friend, a good morning to you too. What is it this time? You want me to assassinate the president?" He chuckled at his own joke.

"Stop fooling around, it's serious Onome."

"Whoa! You sound touchy. What is this about?"

"The Speaker of the House of Assembly just sent me an order to endorse the delivery of radioactive phosphate to a warehouse in Lagos. The order has to be there in one week."

"Jesus!" exclaimed Onome.

"Now you know what's eating me up," finished Tade solemnly.

"Man, I don't envy you at all. I hate to be in your shoes right now. What do you plan to do?"

"I don't know. I am thinking of making enquiries because this whole thing looks suspicious. I want to know if there's any urgent demand for radioactive phosphate by the Science Research Institute that would make the House of Assembly issue such an order."

"Nope. If there was my dear friend, I would be the first to know."

"Then why did they...?"

"Don't overheat your brain Tade," cut in Onome. "It's a strange demand, I admit but you have to do what they want, after all they are the rulers of the country."

"Don't you think I know that?" grumbled Tade, his face settling into a worried frown. "I'll get them the order but I'll send a formal complaint to the president himself. Nobody's going to frame me for what I didn't do."

"Tade, a word of advice here. Don't offend deity, don't annoy divinity. They are a hard lot to deal with."

"I'll remember that pal. I've got to go now. Thanks anyway."

"The pleasure's mine."

He dropped the phone and resumed drumming his fingers on the table, the worried frown not once leaving his face.

⌘ ⌘

As soon as he hung up, Onome Agoro picked up his mobile phone and dialed a number. Almost immediately, someone at the other end picked it up.

"Hello."

"Good morning Sir, it's me Onome. Eh… Sir, Tade Joseph just called in to confirm the order like you said he would."

There was a long pause then the voice spoke again.

"What is he planning to do? Did you find that out?" came the gruff reply.

"Yes Sir, he's planning to investigate and he's threatened to send a letter to the president about the matter."

The inevitable pause. When the voice spoke again it was much calmer, the gruff reply completely gone.

"Don't worry I'll take over from here, ok?"

"Yes Sir."

"Eh… sir, about your promise to…"

"I'll see to it that you are duly compensated."

"Sir, thank you I am glad…"

The line went dead. Onome shrugged, picked up his pen and went back to work.

⌘ ⌘

The radioactive phosphate was delivered but the threatened letter to the president was never written. Two weeks later the body of Tade Joseph was found in a rundown motel on the outskirts of town. A police autopsy report revealed traces of alcohol and a fatal dose of heroin in his system.

CHAPTER 3

Central District, Abuja, 10:09 p.m.

IT WAS A TYPICAL STORMY NIGHT, THE HEAVENS insisted on venting its anger on the earth in torrents of insistent rainfall and thundering.

Reverend Christopher Enebeli sat at his desk, head bent in concentration. The windows of the office rattled in protest at the constant clamoring of the storm outside and the raindrops drumming against the glass kept up a consistent rhythm.

He was planning something big.

Reverend Enebeli had always been a stickler for big planning with an undisguised penchant for manipulating and lobbying when the need presented itself.

At the School of Theology, Akwa, Anambra State where as he put it, he was spiritually initiated into the lucrative world of pastoring, he had been a constant and notable offender. At the slightest provocation from the elders of the College which were the school's power that be, he would whip up 'his team" of hardened supporters and begin to make unrealistic demands of the authorities. One time he had reporters from the Daily Sentinel, a local newspaper outfit, besiege the school authorities over a case of water shortage at the hostel.

He had always been a creature of circumstance.

His umbilical ties to newspaper reporters had over the years been responsible for his unprecedented rise to recognition. After being removed from three churches were he had been assigned, with the last one almost causing a feud amongst the locals of the small community, he decided to forego the small time assemblage of saints and channel his energies into more worthy and rewarding pastoring.

At a dinner organized by an aging and retiring man of God, Pastor Enebeli was called upon to extol the glories of the veteran soldier of the cross. There was only one thing pastor Enebeli could do with unparalleled passion. He could talk, and talk, he did.

Several years later and with several eulogies, political prayers and spiritual lobbying under his belt, Pastor Enebeli had become a force to be reckoned with: with a prestigious office space at the high end of Central District, Abuja and a seven figure bank account.

He was working late today. Shifting in his seat to better distribute the weight of his bulky frame, he reached out for the cup of coffee that was on his mahogany desk. On touching the cold cup, he automatically withdrew his hand and without looking up grunted disapprovingly. The coffee had been made for him by his secretary thirty minutes ago and had been left untouched all the while.

Then he heard it.

The slight almost indistinct sound of dripping water. Pausing momentarily, he listened again.

The storm raged outside drowning all other sound. He bent down to his work mumbling quietly to himself. There was a moment of silence and there it was again; a distinct dripping sound quite clearly heard above the sound of raindrops hitting the pavement outside. Pastor Enebeli had always had excellent hearing and could clearly pick out and sometimes define sounds that others could not hear.

Someone was in the inner office.

"Who's there?" he barked out.

Silence.

"Janet is that you?" he queried.

Silence.

He realized that Janet had gone home about twenty-five minutes ago. Reluctantly he began to get up from behind his desk when the lights in the office suddenly went out throwing the room into total darkness.

He swore under his breath as he searched for a torch. Hitting the cup of coffee on the desk, it went crashing to the floor.

He swore louder.

Groping around inside his desk finally produced a torch and at the same time a sudden realization hit him. The dripping sound had gotten louder and if he wasn't mistaken was coming from directly in front of him.

He froze.

The next moment in a surprisingly quick movement, he spun round pointing the torch at the source of the sound and at the same time switching it on.

The darkness suddenly came alive in the shape of a man. That was all he saw before the torch was roughly knocked out of his hand. He screamed, involuntarily stumbled back, clawing the darkness in a bid to offer some form of defense. With amazing speed the figure leapt over the desk, expertly avoiding the flailing arms and the next thing pastor Enebeli felt was cold steel on his flesh. The way it settled just underneath his Adam's apple and the sharp sting it produced removed all doubt about it being anything else.

It was a knife and razor sharp at that.

The pastor drew in breath fearfully and tried to say something but the words stuck in his throat.

"I am a man of God," he blurted out eventually.

There was a soft laugh from behind him. It almost sounded soothing.

"I know who you are Pastor Enebeli," the voice was soft spoken and calm.

It threw him into renewed panic. Just then a lightning flash momentarily lit the room throwing a brief reflection of the man behind him on the window pane across the room. The face was still obscured in the darkness and could not be seen but the arm that held the wicked looking knife was rippling with muscles and every square inch of it was tattooed.

His lips quivered as he sucked in air noisily and without thinking blurted out.

"The Lord is my shepherd, I shall not want. He maketh me to lie down in green…"

In one quick movement, the knife jerked cutting a neat arc in the throat just below the Adam's apple. The words died in Pastor Enebeli's mouth and a surprised expression replaced the one of fear as blood bubbled out of the slit throat.

The tattooed hand withdrew slowly from the throat to grip the pastor's neck from behind and in one smooth move smashed the face against the mahogany desk.

The thrashing body stood perfectly still.

The intruder left as quietly as he had come.

CHAPTER 4

Niger State, 9:02 a.m.

THERE IS AN ONGOING DEBATE THAT ZUMA ROCK, which is on the outskirts of the Federal Capital Territory, Abuja lies in the very centre of Nigeria.

From the rock itself to the belated commercial capital Lagos, is an approximate distance of 780 kilometers and from it to the northern hemisphere of Maiduguri is a distance of 790 kilometers and 740 kilometers from it to the coastal boundaries of Calabar.

Egunu perched comfortably on the 725 meter high monolith fondly referred to as "Gateway to Abuja" and waited.

Waiting was one thing he could do well.

One time he had waited on the top of a tree in the Congo forests for over twenty-four hours without as much as a stir and eventually his patience had paid off. The elusive prey had finally emerged. A business partner who suddenly had gone AWOL after an alleged embezzlement scam and was holed up in a cabin in the forest. The contract was for a clean job. He smiled wryly to himself, conjuring up the memory of that kill. It was a masterpiece in itself. Hungry and tired after his endless vigilance he had put a bullet clean through the guy's eyes and another closely followed one into his temple. Those were the days.

He was wearing a windbreaker with the hood up and wrap-around sunshades that did a good job of disguising his facial features. No point in being remembered by some nosy holiday people picnicking nearby who would pass on the information to the police. On arrival, he had picked a spot between two jutted rocks, produced his killing gear and arranged himself as comfortably as possible.

The view was breathtaking.

Lazy clouds sailed nearby, slowly parting ways to accommodate the morning sun. If the intelligence given him was on point, then the car would be cruising past in another 20 minutes. He lit a cigarette and studied the layout below through the cross hairs of his military grade sniper rifle. It was a bit windy up here; he noticed and adjusted his rifle for wind interference. The Russian manufactured military rifle Elvinch 6.0 was fashioned to ease the process of delivering death. It had a sniper scope that could pick up a cockroach from a thousand meters and a man's pimple at close to nine hundred. Packaged with infrared vision for night hunting, body heat signature recognition and mercury tipped explosive bullets, it was in high demand amongst black market arms dealers — the ultimate assassin's accessory.

He finished the cigarette, crushed the butt on a nearby rock and put it in the side pocket of his windbreaker. In the relative quiet of the rock, he heard the sound of an approaching vehicle and adjusted his sights for a look. The image of the driver's face jumped at him and slowly shifting to the left, he got his prey in the cross hairs.

It was common practice for Reverend Jaiyesimi Davids, the senior pastor of Rock City assembly church to ride on the passenger seat next to his driver. The intelligence Egunu had gotten was solid. It was one thing to pick off a stationery target but a moving one was not as easy. It involved the complex process of exacting minute movements on a solid grip of the rifle while maintaining the prey in sight. Timing was as important because you never really get a second chance.

He exhaled slowly and squinted into the riflescope.

The bullet exited the silenced rifle with a soft "putt", travelling the distance in-between at lightning speed. Shattering the windscreen of the car, it came to rest between the eyes of Reverend Jaiyesimi Davids, exploding on impact. The car screeched fiercely swerving wildly as fragments of blood and bone splattered all over the driver. It finally crashed into an electric pole with what was left of the Reverend's head resting awkwardly on the driver's lap. The top half of his face was gone.

Egunu smiled.

CHAPTER 5

Kano State, Nigeria, 2:40 p.m.

THE LONE FIGURE STOOD LEANING ON THE WALL OF the house, clutched reverently between both hands was a copy of the Holy Koran. He had been standing like that for three hours anticipating Major Haman Sabo's return. The rise and fall pattern of his chest accompanied by a wheezing sound was a remarkable sight.

Amin Dakaram had kept vigil on this same spot for two days, the guard at the gate had dismissed him saying the Major was out of the country on urgent business and might not return till the weekend but he had remained unperturbed and had quietly volunteered to wait.

He was like a religious apparition. His hair was well grown and dusty in the slowly gathering harmattan haze. His beard was rough and unkempt and he was adorned in a loosely fitted *babariga* dress common to the average northern man that rode safely to his ankle. The Holy Koran was clutched to his midriff and he scowled like a man in pain. On his foot was a simple sandal. He was unlike any other northerner but for his eyes.

They were glazed over and void of any form of life. It was like staring into a dark pool without any ripple. Only an occasional flicker from them gave any indication that it functioned.

Just looking at him it was hard to believe that he had acquired his education in the University of Sussex, London, majoring in Islamic Etiology and Arabic History. A further foray into the study of basic theological recombination had successfully stripped him of all attention from female counterparts leaving him undesired and undesirable.

His silent vigilance finally paid off as he overheard the Major's wife tell the driver to go pick the Major at the airport. He smiled to himself revealing a wrongly arranged dentition, wheezed and burst into a fit of coughing. Reaching into the pocket of his dress, he produced an inhaler and sucked on it animatedly. *This is my moment; no sickness will take away the joy of victory from me.*

He was beyond caring for himself. The plan was what really mattered. *Soon Allah's desires would be fulfilled because the Major was the link to it.*

He had no doubt that the major would embrace the plan. It was simply ingenious. He had seen the look in the Major's eyes as he addressed Muslim delegates from all over the country at Hujaram weekend two months ago. It was a cold reflection of what lay in his own. It was a quest for power. Absolute power. From then on, he had attended every one of the Major's speaking engagement sessions and had known simply that he was the chosen one.

He admitted that the plan was imprecise and needed a few adjustments but in its entirety, it was the answer — Allah's ultimate desire to emancipate all Muslim believers. He dipped his hand into his pocket and clutched the paper he had hidden there. It brought a renewed smile to his face. Another bout of coughing seized him as he bent double racking with pain.

The doctors had insisted he had less than three months to live. Some terminal disease was eating him up inside and the best they could do was offer him a life expiry date. The sickness must have had something to do with his sudden and passionate desire to right some existing wrongs. Some others finding their life expectancy reduced to mere days would have retreated away from life, Amin chose to research life.

⌘ ⌘

The spotlessly clean BMW car, carrying Major Haman Sabo slowed at the gate. The lone figure hurried over to it and drummed on the glass impatiently. The Major glared at the imposter, turned round and glowered at the driver.

"Sir, he's been waiting to see you for two days. He says Allah sent him to you."

"I don't want an audience", was the Major's only reply.

The driver took the cue and drove through as the gate was opened. The figure reacted immediately, flinging himself at the gate screaming and demanding to be heard.

⌘ ⌘

One hour later, the man was still outside. He just could not be ignored. He was relentless; shouting so loud it could be heard all over the street. He was nothing short of insane because of the words he spoke but they were nevertheless compelling. Unconsciously it stirred something deep within the Major's heart. The stranger was going on and on about a certain revolution, saying that Allah had endorsed the fight and that was why he had been sent here, that the Major could not obstruct the destiny of the oppressed Muslims on the streets.

People passing stared at him and some nodded compassionately associating him with the slowly growing mentally inadequate individuals on the streets of Kano.

He was past caring what people thought.

He persisted saying that if the Major was unyielding to Allah's beckoning that he would be discarded and Allah would raise for himself a man courageous enough to fight the cause. He resorted to calling the Major unprintable names, employing obscenities to help make his point.

The fool was drawing a crowd, Major Haman mused, studying the stranger from the security monitor.

Demented fool!

The Major was a man of very few words. He had bulbous bloodshot eyes that seemed to speak without saying a thing, a clean-shaven dome of a head, a huge nose and cavernous mouth that fought equally for prominence. The first reaction he got from any new acquaintance was fear. He grew to like the strange feeling it gave him whenever it happened.

The fool is trying my patience.

The locals had begun to gather. It wasn't everyday that they were blessed with a sight such as this. The stranger began to hurl rocks at the gate of the house as his ranting increased. It wasn't his action that was worrying the Major as much as the words he spoke.

"Sir, what do we do about him?" the driver queried, cutting suddenly into the Major's thoughts.

"Send him in."

⌘ ⌘

It had happened years ago in Asarudin Community Mosque in the poor section of Akwanga district, Jos. They had just concluded the last Salat prayers of the day and the urchins were filing out of the mosque in lines like a human centipede, murmuring and quarreling all the while.

Imam Ibru Yamani, an esteemed Islamic scholar was a no nonsense person who hardly ever spoke except at prayers and not at all to children. It was rumored amongst the children that a look from him could make you say things you would never dream to say to your closest allies.

He was regarded as some sort of enigma of righteousness and had spoken several words of wisdom that with the passing of time had unveiled exactly as said.

As the children breezed past, Imam Ibru suddenly, without warning, set his eyes on nine year old Haman. From the corner of his eyes, Haman caught the look and cringed in fear. The look intensified and it was like the skin on the side of Haman's face was on fire.

What had he done wrong? Did the Imam catch him pinching his friend Ibrahim during prayers? Or had Musa reported him about…

"Haman, come here."

It was at best a hoarse whisper but it carried clearly all over the hall for all to hear. Suddenly and without warning time froze.

⌘ ⌘

The stranger regarded his surroundings quietly. He was obviously spent and his chest heaved up and down trying desperately to keep up with his laboured breathing. He reached again into his pocket and produced his inhaler, brought it to his mouth and inhaled deeply all the while his eyes staying fixed on the Major. The stare had the capacity to intimidate any man but Major Haman was not just any man.

"What do you want from me, stranger?" the Major demanded rudely.

"My name is Amin Dakaram and I believe Allah has sent me to you, Major Haman," he stated calmly. "You are the chosen one."

⌘ ⌘

It was like someone hit a fast forward button. The next thing little Haman knew was that he was standing a few feet from Imam Ibru. He pressed his fingers together, desperately trying to stop them from shaking.

The Imam crouched slowly studying the boy with unveiled interest. He blinked fiercely at the terrified kid, disregarding the small crowd that had converged around them.

"It's you..." He mumbled quietly to himself, "you are the chosen one."

⌘ ⌘

Sitting quietly in the Imam's office an hour later still didn't help little Haman relax. His parents had been summoned and they listened with rapt attention at the Imam's statements.
It was a prophecy like no other.

His mother was already sobbing quietly at the words she was hearing. His father sitting stiffly stared at the Imam stone faced, a shocked expression replacing his regular scowl.

"It might be difficult to comprehend but your son is destined to spawn great evil in this land, leaving death and destruction in his wake. It is his destiny to cause great confusion and fear among his generation. Nobody would be able to stop it."

CHAPTER 6

"YOUR MOVE, LINDA."

She tried to concentrate on the game. It had been on for close to an hour with Professor Mesnavich gaining the upper hand. She squinted at the computer screen and tried to predict his next move. Professor Mesnavich was head of research in the Institute of Biometrics and Concise Analogy, Russia and he also held the current title of grand master in the circles of chess.

Linda Ebachie, thousands of miles away from the grandmaster had tried week after week through the internet to snatch the title off the Professor but it always ended pretty much the same way with Linda being on the losing end and having to endure another session of the Professor's numerous boasts.

Today was no different except for the fact that she just couldn't concentrate. A lot was on her mind. She made a move and immediately regretted it. The Professor burst into raucous laughter, which boomed into the earpiece connected to her computer.

"We are a bit absent minded today, aren't we miss Linda? Is everything all right over there in Nigeria or are you just getting rusty?"

Linda imagined the statement being accompanied by a sneer. She kept a placid expression and stared blankly at the alternating boxes of black and white on the screen as the Professor made his move.

"Checkmate, darling."

The Professor burst into another round of laughter throwing his head back for effect. She logged off her computer in irritation but the echo of his laughter lingered on in her head.

"Bloody bastard," she remarked through clenched teeth.

⌘ ⌘

Linda Ebachie was special. She had been perpetually confined to a wheel chair at the age of twenty due to a hit and run accident. The driver of the vehicle was never apprehended but the vehicle was. A heavy-duty utility truck, with a stainless steel front fender and 500 kilometers on the meter. She had lain bleeding at the scene of the accident, in a secluded area in Ikeja for the better part of an hour. She was in a coma when she was brought in. After series of operations to correct her mangled appendage, the doctors had finally prophesied that she would never walk again.

The accident changed everything.

Her Mother had suffered the most. A series of nervous breakdowns, which she never totally recovered from. After several failed attempts to bring her back to her vibrant self, she was sent to the village to try to recover. She never made it back, dying peacefully in her sleep a few yards from where she was born.

Her father's reaction was surprising. After the appropriate duration of grieving for his wife, he unearthed a secret trust fund that he had kept cleverly hidden from everybody, cashed in on it and went to work summoning past contacts and foreign acquaintances. If his daughter would never walk again, he reasoned, he would make her as comfortable sitting in a wheel chair as anybody else in the world.

She had started quite well, easily excelling in her academics with minimal effort and zero supervision. She was unlike her peers who chose to taunt themselves on the latest fashion craze and were content with sampling the pack of new teenage boys delivered to the school each year.

She was only interested in one thing — academics. To say she was addicted to her books would be putting it mildly. She read everything she came across and never forgot a word of it. She was, as her father playfully put it, the ninth undiscovered wonder of the world.

"You would make a very lucky man proud someday," he often teased beaming with approval.

Theirs was a well to do family and a happy one as well. Her earliest memories were of her father's booming infectious laughter and his poor imitation of Shakespeare which never failed to make mother laugh even when she was upset with him. Her father had a huge library in the house that contained an impressive collection of books ranging from human cloning to military armory. It was a well stocked and vast collection. Linda at the age of six loved to accompany her father to the library. There was a tingling presence in the room that reminded her of a church cathedral. She would stare at the books hearing their silent invitation to come discover the knowledge that lay in their depths. It quickly became her favorite pastime, just sitting in the library and leafing through the books.

"Where's Linda?" her mother would ask. "I've been looking for her ever since she came back from school."

"She's in the library sampling the beauties of wisdom. Actually she's reading a book on the history of England."

"If I find her in there, I'll teach her the history of naughty girls!" her mother would threaten, brandishing a spoon or any other kitchen utensil.

"But she's only…"

Her mother's legendary scowl always did the trick.

⌘ ⌘

The principal's letter had a very strict, official tone to it. It was a request for Linda's parents to come see her at the school urgently. It was all Linda's father could do to restrain his wife from interrogating Linda about the letter.

"Patience, my dear. We would know what it's all about by Monday." He had said.

First thing Monday morning they were both seated at the principal's office. The principal, Mrs. Amah Okunobi was a sight to behold. Ramrod stiff and sitting upright on the chair as if comfort was a luxury she could not bring herself to indulge in. Her hair was pulled back in a fierce bun and tightly packed with no strand out of place. She wore thick-rimmed glasses that made her eyes look like boiled eggs. There were crease lines around her small mouth as she spoke.

"Your daughter Linda has a problem," she intoned gravely. Both parents adjusted themselves self-consciously on their seats expecting the worse.

Was it a case of unruly conduct, teenage vice, a pregnancy scandal?

Even as the parents considered the varying options, they knew it was unlike their Linda. Her only passion was…

"She's too brilliant for her class."

⌘ ⌘

The wheelchair when it was finally delivered to the Ebachie residence was state of the art and high tech. For months, Linda and her father had debated and argued on the specifications to be included in the mechanism. With a satellite guided communication system, an updated worldwide GPS locator, a holographic off screen voice activated super computer and a methane fueled Z-99 mini engine, it was the very first of its kind.

She immediately dug into the manual.

CHAPTER 7

KOME OGENE HAD GRADUATED SUMMA CUM LAUDE, a feat that as he boasted to anyone who cared to listen was effortless. From the time when he could differentiate girls from boys by their protruding shirtfronts, he had been a non-conformist. Always of the opinion that the entire system was a psychological virus and those in authority merely modern slave drivers. One of his university lecturers had described him as a first class mind on a prodigal frame. After unsuccessfully deploying his unpopular beliefs to his primary school colleagues in a bid to clinch the post of head boy and losing the post by a startling figure of one hundred and forty two votes, Kome finally understood.

The system was not ready for a phenomenon like him. He was an intellectual deity set above average minions.

I don't need them, they need me.

Fortified by this reasoning he set out to prove he was the best.

With nothing but a well-used antenna, a small wavelength circuit board and choice wires he, at the age of 12, patched into a global digital satellite TV network and saved his parents the subscription fee. His introduction to the world of computers upgraded his delinquent skills and opened him up to a broader perspective of digital debauchery. He was hacking into major "secure" networks at 13 and at 15 had unrestricted access to over a thousand credit card information worldwide.

The secure world of digital communication began to take notice but it was not until his most daring digital achievement did they sit up. The federal allocation for the month of May 2010 to be distributed amongst the three tiers of government in Nigeria amounted to N403.3b. It was lodged safely in a government approved CBN account awaiting its collection by the parties involved. By a series of illegal access and complex wire transfers, the better part of the money ended up in an untraceable account somewhere in Mexico belonging of course to Kome. The outcry that followed was transposed into a dangerous climax that threatened both life and limb when the media splattered it all over and dubbed it "the biggest fraud factor of the year". Those supposedly responsible for "the loss" were rounded up, questioned and tortured but the authorities got no nearer to the truth.

An expert computer analyst from the US government was finally requested for and a digital investigation commenced. The transfer was done by using a series of IP addresses engineered by a code that shuffled and altered them as soon as they were pinpointed. It was clearly the work of a professional. The search took nearly two months before the correct IP address was finally located and pinned down. Kome Ogene became a federal fugitive after the SSS located his residence and ransacked the place. Almost immediately, he went off the radar and remained untraceable for two years before, by a stroke of luck and some carelessness on his part, he was apprehended. One of his girl friends stole and swiped one of his many credit cards in a "monitored" supermarket in Abuja. The transaction showed up at the SSS headquarters and ten minutes later the unsuspecting girl was in the hands of the police. After that, Kome wasn't hard to find. He was apprehended at his secret rendezvous still in a bath towel and surrounded by half a dozen super computers and enough sensitive intelligence to start another civil war.

CHAPTER 8

20 Years Ago. Kano, September 1992.

ALMADIN UMARU FLED THROUGH SURROUNDING forest areas avoiding villages as much as he could with the purse clutched to his side with one hand. Thick bushes slashed at him leaving painful wound marks on his skin as dark clouds of doubts assailed his mind.

They deserved it!

He wasn't to blame for his employer's unholy conduct so Allah was probably in support of his actions, he reasoned. Reaching a small hill he paused momentarily, looking around and then he was off again.

⌘ ⌘

An average Almajiri urchin has a resolute die-hard disposition to life. He attacks it with an attitude, taking its meager offerings as God sent. He expects no more than he can comfortably carry and offers in exchange commensurate labour to that effect. Almadin Umaru had lived in the Tsangaya School for more than two years without incident. He was one of the many offspring in the streets of Kano who had plagued the society with unanswered questions and the government with unresolved manifestoes. Left by their poor parents to acquire the required Islamic knowledge and most importantly fend for themselves, they had slowly transformed into hardened societal castaways.

Almadin was fortunate. He was entitled to some food and a little money if he could perform chores at the Muram residence on a daily basis. His lot was considerably better than his other colleagues who were not so fortunate to have a standby employer and had to flood the streets soliciting from strangers. This made it easy for him to pay up his *Kudin sati*, the midweek tax imposed on all Almajiri scholars by their teachers. Over the weeks, he had grown attached to the Murams, majorly because they filled his belly with food and also because Mallam Muram's wife always spoke kind words to him.

Nobody else ever did.

Especially not his parents whom he had not seen for over two years now. At 8 years old he was tall for his age, light skinned with hooded sunken brown eyes, prominent cheekbones and a penchant for work that would shame a full time labourer.

His employer's wife, Abike Muram was a woman to be loved, so Almadin loved and respected her. He would watch her from the corner of his eyes clad in a colorful hijab as she supervised the affairs of the kitchen. She would stop by occasionally and pat his head playfully.

Allah could not have made anything more glorious, he reasoned.

Almadin noticed that her husband Mallam Muram was never around.

What other pressing matters could a husband have to attend to that would warrant his abandoning an angel like this?

⌘ ⌘

He had been running for close to two hours. His legs were weary and his breath came out in ragged bursts.

I have to rest.

He was spent with fatigue and besides, from what he could see nobody was coming after him. He finally stopped under a large tree and resting his back on it sat on the ground. He looked at his palm and cringed. There were specks of blood on them. He hurriedly gathered some sand and rubbed them roughly on his palm to remove the blood.

⌘ ⌘

Almadin had first seen the woman when he was gathering firewood for the kitchen. She was slim and graceful with polished smooth skin, cat like eyes and a haughty manner. He disliked her instantly. Who was she and why was she in the kitchen cooking? He had finally decided to avoid her like a plague after being burned by her temper a few times.

He finally got some answers to his questions about the new woman.

He was delivering some dried clothes into Mallam Muram's bedroom when he walked into her and the Mallam entangled in a love embrace. Standing transfixed to the spot, he watched the Mallam excitedly remove her clothes and caress her breasts.

He had lost it instantly.

The next thing he knew was that he was fleeing the Muram residence with a money pouch, leaving behind two half-naked dead bodies covered in their own blood.

⌘ ⌘

Almadin Umaru had returned years later to the city of Kano a different person. The only place he remembered clearly was the location of the Tsangaya School. He had been gone that long.

The school was no longer standing. A group of beggars assailed the entrance of the run down structure and kept guard over its miserly remains. Almadin crossed the dusty road to a shanty restaurant nearby and after careful inquiries was told that the school had been shut down by Childcare International and the aged Mallam in charge was in the government hospital at Kawa.

The hospital was a medical anomaly with stained walls and an offensive antiseptic aroma that clung to everyone. The Mallam was in the intensive care unit when Almadin walked in. His bony structure was sharply outlined in the remains of his flesh and at intervals he made a gurgling sound like a man drowning. The equipment that surrounded him keeping him connected to life beeped intermittently. Almadin stared at the stationary figure on the bed and eventually bent over the body of the man who had first taught him the principles of Islam. The stench was overpowering, a mixture of human sweat and rotting flesh. His eyes flickered slowly and focused unseeing on the torn ceiling boards above.

"My teacher, I have brought my *Kudin sati.*" He whispered softly into the man's ears.

The lifeless figure drew in breath sharply and smiled a crooked smile.

⌘ ⌘

Thirty minutes later, Almadin left the hospital. The bond between teacher and student, instructor and scholar was ageless and unending. The Mallam had not forgotten his student; in fact, he had constantly offered prayers for his safety. When the police had finally come to the school to apprehend Almadin on the death of Mallam Muram and his new wife, the teacher had fended them off expertly. They had returned weeks later with a court injunction by Childcare International to close up the school and an arrest warrant for the Mallam. He had been herded off to court and accused of training children terrorists and having links to terrorist groups. Unwilling to "co-operate" with the authorities, he was thrown into prison and quickly forgotten until years later when a new administration, willing to please, had released all outstanding prisoners of the state.

Almadin remembered everything like it was only yesterday; how he had fled to the Mallam after the incident shaking uncontrollably. The Mallam had made an instant decision; tearing a piece of paper, he scribbled an address and handed it to the child.

"Find this address child; explain everything and you will be safe."

That was how the journey had begun.

CHAPTER 9

THE ASO ROCK PENITENTIARY SERVICE OFFICIALLY did not exist. There was no steel protected state-of-the-art bunker twenty feet below the home of the Nigerian president that catered to "prisoners of the state". It was not documented anywhere and if it was ever brought up, would be quickly denied and brushed aside as the ranting of a science fiction fanatic. However, it in fact existed and was known to only a privileged few. The closely guarded secret was passed on to newly sworn in presidents and came to be known as "the will'. Buried underneath the renowned Aso Rock edifice, the Penitentiary Service housed the most politically sensitive and notorious offenders of the state — men and women who carried sensitive intelligence in their heads that if ever released would topple governments and crumble political dynasties. They consisted of a consortium of ex-statesmen, elite politicians and other choice individuals previously loyal to the state but by the communal instinct of self-preservation had been caught with their hands in the pie. Releasing them to regular confinement would entail two things: a loss of their expertise and relevance which was yet in demand and their inevitable exposure to both rival and ally nations who would be willing to pay a substantial sum for what the "patriots" knew. The solution was to extract the state offenders from regular life and isolate them under the nose of the authorities to serve their time and their country in relative peace. It was in this isolated high profile detention facility that Kome Ogene, state offender and hacker extraordinaire was accommodated, after he was relieved of the pleasures of regular living. The entrance requirement was a 15-minute surprisingly friendly prison orientation followed by a medical examination that included a series of injections and a final orientation that doubled as a warning.

Kome remembered clearly the warning because it was given by a mouse-like man with badly crossed eyes and a weird smile yet it carried enough menace to put the fear of God in any man.

"You have been injected with a rare amalgam of lithium and uranium deposits known as cretin that latched onto your central nervous system after only five minutes. The beauty of the mixture is that it intercepts and relays minute pulses of information that co-ordinates your every day reflexes. What I am trying to say is that we now have control of your bodily impulses and anatomic responses and can transmit it when and how we feel." The man paused for effect and smiled when he got none.

"You have been accorded the rights to the pleasures that you are used to in the outside world and any other comfort that you so desire but if you ever attempt to escape this facility, we will not hesitate to shut you down." The smile this time was laced with a hint of a sneer.

"There are a number of things we can do to you with this wonder drug. We can shut the use of your diaphragm, suffocating and killing you in seconds, maybe stop the flow of blood to your heart or do any of a thousand things". This time he chuckled silently then stopped suddenly and frowned theatrically.

"My candid advice to you my guests," the irritating chuckle resumed accompanied by a mock bow.

"Please, give us a chance to use it."

The orientation was over.

CHAPTER 10

THE CHIEF PRIEST OF THE BENIN KINGDOM AND AN impressive array of choice spiritualists were gathered at the city's civic centre with the blessings of the Oba of Benin who was in attendance. The purpose of the gathering was to firmly criticize the recent onslaught of killing of pastors in the state and offer spiritual incantations to finally purge the state of the miscreants perpetrating the misdeed. The dynamics of spiritual cleansing was one held in high regard in Benin City so hundreds of locals were gathered for the rare occasion shaking their heads in pity for the offenders who were soon to be on the receiving end of it. In the midst of the proceedings, the Nigeria Police was tactfully condemned for its ineffective handling of the recent killings in the state and in extension the whole country.

Choice spiritual paraphernalia were brought and brandished, jingled and jostled, oaths were uttered and incantations offered by an ageing chief priest who was clad in nothing but an off-white loin cloth and massive beadings around his neck, waist and ankle. The press was present in all their glory capturing the proceedings to be plastered all over the papers the next day.

As the spiritual cleansing continued, an aide appeared by the side of the Oba, whispered a few words into his ears and he stiffened noticeably. Another killing had just taken place a few kilometers from the very place where they were positioned. This time the man of God in question was a childhood friend of the Oba. His head had been roughly severed from his body and carefully placed on top of the glass pulpit of his church.

The Oba bit his lip in anger drawing blood as he endured the rest of the cleansing ritual.

⌘ ⌘

A curfew was declared in Enugu State after the seventh killing and so by 4 p.m. the streets of the state were totally deserted. Economic analysts argued loud and long that the move was an economic disaster and would eventually cripple the revenue accruing potentials of the state but the executives of the Pentecostal Fellowship of Nigeria had sustained a media outcry that had informed the decision. Their members were dying senselessly.

⌘ ⌘

A three-day city wide peaceful protest, complete with banners and placards, was declared in Ogun State to renounce the ongoing slaughter of pastors. At the end of the three day protest, unsuspecting police officers were rounded up by angry locals and thoroughly beaten for their continued inefficiency.

⌘ ⌘

An animated talk show host in Lagos State passionately claimed on his TV show that it was an obvious Al Qaeda conspiracy to rid the country of all notable Christian leadership. A few opinionated contributors called into the show to mirror the host's point of view.

⌘ ⌘

In a dimly lit top floor office at Abuja, a lone figure put off the LED TV on the wall and smiled. It was happening. The wheels of chaos were turning. It was time for the next phase of the plan.

We need to activate the A-Men committee.

CHAPTER 11

THERE ARE ABOUT TWENTY KNOWN BUS STOPS between the densely populated Mile Two axis and the famous Ojota Motor Park of Lagos State. All birthed by situational consequence but over time sanctioned by the masses. Korede Odunade alighted at "Cemetery Bus Stop" opposite the meat market and slowly made his way to the courthouse across the road.

The morning's proceedings would be as always, lifeless and without zest. A domestic dispute gone legal, a cut and dry criminal case with no witnesses or evidence whatsoever, an alleged car smuggling ring conspiracy that was nearly two years old and without an indictment. Korede chuckled softly as he ran through his mind the limited possibilities of a regular courthouse day. It was the unique structure of the Nigerian legal system that produced such cases, he often commented. Nothing else like it the world over. The "official allocation" given him by the Department of Public Prosecution of Lagos State, whom, as he put it was his employer and empowerer, was a 20 by 10 feet rat hole that was shared by six other lawyers with no personal space belonging to anyone. It was a series of well-used tables and chairs jumbled together with labeled boxes on the floor to contain filed cases. The red files were for already treated cases and the green files were for pending ones. A black file was a death sentence but it was seldom seen.

Korede had always wanted to be a lawyer and so had obliged himself, plunging into it headfirst. When his friends ventured into more lucrative legal sectors like property and entertainment law, Korede stubbornly stuck to the age long enterprise of prosecution. Defiant in his defense that it was an overlooked sector that deserved capable hands, he, despite multiple counsels, went on. Two years after law school, having worked exhaustively at the Department of Public Prosecution, with nothing substantial to show for it but an unrewarded loyalty to the state, he had come to regret his lofty ideals. It was half a decade too late.

⌘ ⌘

The office was abuzz with talk about the latest religious killings that the press had sensationally dubbed "the slaying of God's servants". The word going round was that the Nigerian Bar Association through the office of the Director of Public Prosecution was releasing a strongly worded four-page letter to the Federal Executive Council, the National Assembly and some choice media houses, condemning the helplessness of the presidency in "apprehending a few local terrorists that had decided to hold the nation to ransom".

Five seasoned petitioners had created the draft and a veteran committee of prosecutors had sharpened it further. A press conference was slated that weekend to further air their grievances at the nonchalance of the authorities.

Korede walked into the office reading a newspaper and abruptly stopped in his tracks. The office was strangely quiet.

He looked up from his newspaper and regarded his colleagues. Something was definitely wrong. Everyone was staring at him. *Did something happen?*

Someone spoke up finally.

"Oga wants you in his office immediately."

⌘ ⌘

Korede had only been in the top floor office once and that was to defend a colleague against an official query he was erroneously given. *What have I done to require a summon?*

He sighed, braced himself and walked into the office. Three high-ranking members of the Nigerian Bar Association were seated in some sort of meeting. They studied him openly as he walked in.

"You are Barrister Korede Odunade?"

"Yes I am sir."

"We need your help."

⌘ ⌘

The more they talked to Korede, the more tensed he got. They were planning an affront at the government as regards the recent killings in the country and wanted a front man to spearhead the protests.

More like a person to take the fall should anything go wrong.

The only good part of the plan was that he had been unanimously chosen.

CHAPTER 12

THE AUTOPSY REPORTS OF THE DEAD PASTORS AS they came in were similar except for one strange irregularity. About half the number of the murdered victims had strange looking pebbles carefully stuffed into their mouths. They each had seven in number. The pebbles were first screened for DNA and when nothing came up, they were sent over to the Science Research and Development Institute for further analysis.

The Science Research and Development Institute in Abuja is a cathedral-like building with ornamental arches and huge pillars painted in startling off-white. At first glance, it looks like a university edifice but a foray within its walls tells otherwise. Inside of the institute, rock and soil analysis is carried out in the Geoformatics department. That was where the pebbles from the religious killings were sent.

After an hour of centrifuge separation and solvent surface abrasion, the results were out. Strangely, the pebbles were not of an indigenous nature, they were uncommonly like a sample from a small city in faraway Saudi Arabia.

⚜ ⚜

"What was a pebble that is supposed to have originated from Saudi Arabia doing at the scene of a number of religious killings in Nigeria?" Agent Goke Davids asked himself aloud. *Was it possible that the killings had a connection with Saudi Arabia or someone out there wanted them to think it had? They owed it to the victim's families to at least investigate the Saudi Arabian lead.*

He lit his pipe cupping the flame from the match with his left hand and blew furiously as he considered the endless possibilities. *If Saudi Arabia were involved, at what level would it be? Was it a plot by free thinking terrorists or a much deeper conspiracy?*

He stared at his smoking pipe, frowning at the scratch marks by its side.

His father had used this same pipe when Goke was just a boy and would recount stories of his military escapades in the Biafran War; both imaginary and true.

Goke had learnt how to just sit and stare at the breathing pipe slowly cutting out the rest of the world when he wanted to. It had worked while listening to his father's tales and had never failed him not even when he inherited the pipe at his father's death. In his late thirties with a handsome face that never failed to make the hearts of girls flutter, an athletic physique that spoke of years of conditioned sporting and a tribal mark that immediately revealed his parentage. He had been informed by ardent admirers over the years that he was a complete package.

Goke Davids had always been fascinated by law enforcement and the power behind it. At age nine, he wrote in an essay that he wanted to become a police officer, carry a big gun and chase out all the street miscreants in the country. He had finally decided to pursue law enforcement when he discovered that in spite of his father's many accounts of the Biafran War, the old man never saw a day of proper battle. He was safely tucked behind an administrative desk and had only heard the war stories.

Goke, after a degree in psychology had made a grand entrance into the Nigeria Police Academy. He was abducted by the SSS after only a short time because of his exemplary skills in rounding up criminals by applying incredibly accurate deductive reasoning. The crown of his budding career came when as field operations director of the SSS Western Zone, by painstaking and instinctive investigating, he apprehended the most elusive criminal offender of the century; the renowned computer fraudster, Kome Ogene.

By that singular achievement his career had sky rocketed, so he wasn't exactly surprised when his director at the behest of the Minister of Internal Security had put him on this particular case.

Goke left the station and headed on foot for the bus stop. People glanced strangely at him as he passed them. It wasn't commonplace on the streets of Lagos for a young man to smoke a pipe. A few even pointed and laughed.

If I wanted a group of indigenous persons killed, how do I get in contact with someone qualified enough to get the job done professionally? Using a foreigner would be out of the question. Too conspicuous. A local had to have been contracted. Ex-military personnel? Violence had been employed in half of the killings that made it seem personal and not just professional in nature. The other half was professionally executed with limited gore and blood. Was it not possible that two different people did the killings? If that was so then it would explain why half of the victims had pebbles stuffed in their mouths and the other half did not. We need to pursue that line of thought some more and investigate its possibility.

"Ikeja Under Bridge" as it is commonly referred to was nearly deserted by this time of the night. The street traders had packed up their remaining wares and were long gone. A few aspiring miscreants were still gathered around, considering the dwindling possibility of earning some more dishonest living before total darkness obscured their chances. Agent Goke perched on an overturned drum and blew furiously at his pipe squinting at the smoky haze as it slowly rose.

Why go all out and kill pastors thereby risk being discovered as an anti-Christian setup if you were unwilling to claim responsibility for the killings in the first place? Why the lack of subtlety in execution and then make no public statement? It didn't make sense to start with. There is something missing that I cannot put my finger on. The motive for the killings was still unclear and sadly, it was the link to nailing the bastards who perpetrated the plan.

Known Islamic factions around the country were being pulled in for questioning and they had all denied the existence of such a plan. One veteran jihadist had spat in the interrogators face and called the recent events "the retribution of Allah".

CHAPTER 13

ALMADIN CROUCHED UNNOTICED ON THE TOP OF the roof and studied his surroundings. The adversaries were getting more cautious, he noticed. There were six security men stationed around the perimeter of the church, two had guns. He adjusted his position silently on the roof and putting a one-eyed binocular to his eye scanned the inside of the church. The subject was inside presiding over some kind of service with about a thousand members in attendance.

This was going to be fun.

The followers of the infidels need to understand that their religious deities were mere men and that all they have fed them were lies spawn in deceit. Retribution would be delivered tonight in front of them all by Allah's Caliph.

My Son, Muslims have been called by God to establish a righteous and humane political and social order on earth. The only way to live gratefully as Allah's Caliphs is to make full use of the gifting he has bestowed on you.

He began to move, running swiftly in the darkness of the rooftop on rubber soled shoes. His muscles twitched underneath the black tunic he wore as he mouthed the simple words he had heard a thousand times from his Mujahedeen.

Jihad is considered the sixth Pillar of Islam, and thus a form of worship or service to Allah.

He dropped silently on the east side of the church in-between the flower beds and snaked through the children's section, paused at the entrance and looked back. No one had noticed him.

You are an extension of the right arm of Allah. His messenger of death and vengeance. The promise of retribution to those who do not believe.

Almadin drew out his sword and with head bowed mouthed softly the ancient Arabic pronouncement. *Allah Akbar.*

⌘ ⌘

He had never forgotten that night. Arriving finally at the address his teacher had given him after a two day run through the forest, cleverly avoiding police checkpoints and road barricades. he was bruised and bloodied but still clutched the money pouch to his slowly heaving chest. The house was an old obscure cabin made of rock and wood, located on the outskirts of the state and surrounded by dense foliage. It had taken Almadin nearly two hours to locate it. Very exhausted, he had collapsed at the entrance of the house after knocking and blacked out as a figure opened the door.

In the passing days, the occupants of the house had tended him with herbs and food that revived him. He was taken in with no questions asked and became a student of what he later learned was an ancient secret fraternity known simply as "Darl-Al-Harb" which roughly translated means "the house of war".

⌘ ⌘

The messenger of death burst into the church and in a crouch-like run made for the altar. The proceedings prematurely altered, members of the congregation all stared in shock at the figure clad from top to bottom in black as he moved like the wind. The pastor whose hands were raised in midair in an attempt to bless the piece of bread, which he clutched reverently, stared stupefied as the nocturnal figure closed the distance between them.

The power behind every blow is intensified by the passion in your heart my son. You have much passion so your blows would be legendary but you must learn to strike with purpose.

In one smooth motion, Almadin, using the sword like a spear, held it pointed straight with one hand and using the palm of the other hand drove it through the heart of the pastor. The pastor toppled over in shock and hit the ground, gulping in air greedily. A sickening crunch of breaking bone accompanied the removal of the sword and blood spurted uncontrollably from the punctured heart.

A startled gasp went up in the congregation, as pandemonium broke loose. Somebody screamed uncontrollably. Another fainted. Some people made for the altar while others went for the entrance.

Almadin bent over the still thrashing figure, carefully stuffed the mouth with seven smooth stones and disappeared in the commotion.

CHAPTER 14

277 MILES TO THE NORTH OF MECCA LIES THE TOMB of Prophet Muhammad. Contrary to the widespread medieval notion that the resting place of the great Prophet was at Mecca and that the tomb of the Prophet of Islam is suspended in mid-air by lodestones, it lay quietly and unceremoniously in Medina. A mile to the east of the renowned tomb was a gravel heap site of the finest pebbles in the city. A utility truck marked with a crescent moon logo and an inscription in Arabic was parked nearby and two labourers were busy shovelling the pebbles into the truck for the upcoming Hajj Pilgrimage.

⌘ ⌘

As part of the ancient and holy ceremonies of the Hajj, millions of pilgrims from all over the world converged at Medina where they in turn cast pebbles against three large stone pillars representing Satan, as a symbol of the eternal battle that must be waged against the demons within.

⌘ ⌘

At King Abdulaziz International Airport check-in, Saudi Arabia, the airport security official finished prying open the aluminum containers and frowned uncomprehending.

"What are these?" he queried suspiciously in his limited English.

Almadin smiled sweetly and picking up a few of the pebbles in his palm replied. "They are rock samples from the city of the prophet. I am a geologist."

CHAPTER 15

THE A-MEN COMMITTEE HAD BEEN INSTITUTED IN utmost secrecy.

It had taken Major Haman all of one year to put together a secret file of possible conspirators. It consisted of visionary men who were not afraid to take the unpopular route to achieve a greater good and who most importantly had the resources to do so. They were at the heights of their various careers because they had employed radical means to get there — men and women who had everything to gain and everything to lose. Each candidate had been bugged and closely studied for months, both at home and in their offices. Their correspondence, purchase patterns, political affiliations, sexual orientation, business structure antecedent and contacts were properly scrutinized and detailed. Major Haman knew their secrets and weaknesses and was ready to exploit them where and when necessary. They were from different works of life but there was only one thing common to them all, they were all radical practicing Muslims. At the opportune time, they were discreetly contacted and propositioned cautiously.

The bait was irresistible.

Major Haman informed them that for the past eight months, clandestine meetings had been held with heavy investors from the Middle East who were ready to do business with the country's top entrepreneurs only and only if the nation's principles were Islam-based or at least its Christian affiliations were less conspicuous. Billions were primed to be invested in all sectors but they were unwilling to trade on any other terms. The plan that Major Haman had created was to meet those terms head on.

Two of the eight candidates had declined vehemently and months later had met with unfortunate "accidents". One had drowned in his million-naira swimming pool one night and the other a month later had died of food poisoning at an elite bachelor's party.

The other conspirators were careful not to ever meet in person or directly contact each other and with good reason because at the height of their carefully structured careers, it was too dangerous to be connected together. Finally, the meetings had begun.

The agenda was tabled explicitly at the beginning and with military precision, a plan had followed. The plan was in two parts, the first was to create an untraceable nationwide religious scandal, and the next part was to use massive media propaganda to promote a subtle warning to the remaining Christian extremists still in the country. The members had quickly employed their unending resources both legal and otherwise to contract two professionals who could for a substantial reward do the job and at the same time stay off the radar. At the end of the first meeting, just before the specialized communication ear pods each member had inserted in their ears was disconnected, Major Haman had proposed a name for the project.

"As some of you may know, there is a Christian term that is of Hebrew origin and widely used by them today. The term is known as "Amen" and simply put means, "let it be so". My fellow visionaries, I propose with a hint of irony that the project be code-named, 'Operation A-men'."

CHAPTER 16

THE NIGERIAN STATE SECURITY SERVICE SINCE ITS inception in 1986 has been tagged a number of unwholesome aliases ranging from being a private secret police force to cater for political loyalists, to it being an agency for political repression, but no critic has ever disputed its efficiency in abducting the so called "offenders of the state".

Two official-looking vehicles pulled up quietly at the Ebachie residence in Surulere. Mr. Joseph Ebachie was tending the small garden at the back of the house, a pastime he had developed after his wife's death. A radio was blaring nearby. Three dark suited men suddenly burst into the house, took the unsuspecting father out with a well-applied pistol butt to the head and carried both father and struggling daughter into the waiting car outside. They left as quickly as they had come.

Later, eyewitness accounts described the cars used for the abduction as a well used Toyota Camry and a dark coloured Explorer. It wasn't much to go on because Toyota Camrys and Explorers are the most registered vehicles in the Lagos metropolis.

CHAPTER 17

TWO MEN SAT HUDDLED TOGETHER IN THE downstairs bar of the Federal Palace Hotel, Lagos. One was a senior official of the SSS and was dressed stiffly in an oversized suit and checkered tie. The other man, young and intense, was from some obscure government parastatal and had introduced himself simply as a Federal Executor. This was their third meeting; the first two had been a cautious proposition where introductions and details had been minimal in case the proceedings went bad.

The "Federal Executor" had surprising inside knowledge of the workings of the SSS and knew that the senior official he had contacted was the departmental head of a very secretive and unofficial arm of the SSS that was in charge of clandestine government operations. After the first meeting, they both knew they were professionals in their various fields and had thoroughly investigated each other so the verbal banter and denials had been cut to a minimum.

The Federal Executor representing a far "bigger fish" who wasn't interested in trading on a name basis had made a proposition that was as incriminatingly scary as it was simple. He wanted for a staggering sum of money, the names and schedules of the computer security analysts of the Aso Rock Penitentiary Service.

Only a few men alive could lay claim to knowing that such a penitentiary service even existed.

That had been almost a month ago. Both stakeholders had parted not sure if the "consignment" could be delivered but nevertheless were willing to risk it.

The SSS official had finally called after 26 days and requested a meeting. He went straight to the point.

"I have acquired it." He began almost in a whisper after the waiter had served them both.

The Federal Executor stared at the remains of the brandy in his glass and blinked thoughtfully giving no reply.

The SSS official leaned forward and taking from his suit pocket a flash drive, he pushed it across the table at the younger man before leaning back.

"You have about two weeks before the schedule changes again."

⌘ ⌘

Kome Ogene was bent over a book when the janitor entered his "cell". For the 4-month period he had been here, he had only seen a computer once. The SSS had stormed his cell and ordered an IP trace of a computer used by an internet hacker to access credit card info from a CBN database. His blood had raced as his fingers went to work. It was the job of an amateur; nothing near what he could do. The scammer had used an octagon hydra-headed virus to create a glitch on the bank website while using a back access to get at the credit card info.

A foolish and outdated tactic.

Kome had simply created a sterilized portal through the glitch and pinged the IP address used. From then on, it was easy. A back trace on a "pinged IP" when you had a super computer at your disposal was a piece of cake. The scammer was in the police net by nightfall. After his expertise was fully exploited, he had been abandoned again.

Damned parasites!

He studied the busy janitor over the pages of the book on cryptography that he was reading. He was a little surprised when he first started staying here that the janitors usually never spoke; not even when spoken to. They just shuffled around the room doing their cleaning and were never drawn to converse with the "inmates". He soon got to understand why. They never spoke because they could not speak. The Aso Rock Penitentiary service only used janitors that were certified mute; unable to speak. He had laughed loud and long at the realization.

The crafty bastards. Not willing to chance any inmate divulging state secrets.

The janitor in his room was acting rather weird. He was taking minute glances at the tiny closed circuit cameras in the room while working.

How long does it take to dust a simple bookshelf?

Finally, he left and Kome waited a while before approaching the bookshelf. He scanned the mahogany surface that held his limited collection of books and at first didn't notice anything but a more thorough search revealed it. Scrawled hurriedly on the side of the wooden shelf using a blunt object was a simple message.

"14-07-12, 7:30 pm, Manfredi Nicoletti."

CHAPTER 18

IT HAD TAKEN ALMOST TWO HOURS TO SUCCESSFULLY move the distraught congregation out of the church premises. It was a slow exodus of mourners that were unwilling to part with the dead body of their pastor; not when the slaughter had taken place right before their eyes. Women wailed uncontrollably and flung themselves on the altar and the dead body, destroying any hope of gathering forensic evidence. They were quickly herded outside the church gate where another crowd had gathered.

Agent Goke squatted over the body and studied it closely. There was no doubt that it was the work of the religious assassin. The victim was lying in a pool of his own blood with an ugly looking gash on the left side of his chest. His face was contorted in an expression of agony and from his half-open mouth was the inevitable pebbles, neatly packed inside.

Crazy bastard.

The forensic team were on their way, they were the best the country could offer; a loan from the SSS. Agent Goke was sure they would find nothing as was the case with the other bodies.

No fingerprints.

No DNA sample.

Nothing to work with.

Outside, police officers were taking accounts from several witnesses calm enough to give it and agent Goke scanned the church premises thoughtfully. He produced his pipe, lit it slowly and inhaled the first instalment of acrid smoke deeply.

"I can recognize him."

Agent Goke turned round and came face to face with the person who had spoken. He regarded the man who was in his late thirties, darkly handsome with an expression of someone who had seen it all. He was smartly dressed in a shirt and a tie that was slightly loosened.

Office worker.

"I saw his face clearly and can recognize him anywhere," He repeated in earnest, scowling all the while.

"Are you sure?" Agent Goke queried cautiously. The young man could be suffering from shock at seeing his pastor butchered right before him.

He nodded quickly, the blue and red siren lights from the parked police cars nearby flickering in patterns on his frowning face.

"Follow me."

Barrister Korede quickly followed the young police officer outside to his parked car and slumped on the passenger seat blinking repeatedly.

Agent Goke stared at the man in his car for close to a minute.

"Talk to me."

⌘ ⌘

Barrister Korede stared at the agent in front of him and grimaced. The questioning had been going on for close to two hours and he was spent. This was the third agent relentlessly asking the same questions with little or no alteration. Korede tapped his fingers impatiently on the metal table in front of him and waited for the agent to start the routine of studying him quietly before the questioning would begin. After the required period of observation the questioning finally started.

"Did the killer have any form of facial marks or any other recognizable feature?"

"No, he didn't."

"Skin colour?"

"Light brown."

He paused dramatically and scribbled something into a writing pad as if light brown was a colour tone that was totally new to him.

"Are you sure, Sir?"

"Positive."

"Type and colour of clothing."

"Black tunic, Arabian style."

He scribbled that down also and stared at it thoughtfully like it would provide some new insight.

"Please describe him Sir."

Korede sighed audibly and slid lower in the uncomfortable metal chair. *Here we go again.*

"Average height, muscular with an athletic physique, fair skinned with ...eh... prominent cheek bones."

"I see," he muttered as he scribbled some more.

"Was there anything strange about the way he acted?"

"Apart from his killing a pastor in cold blood?"

The agent stared fixedly not seeing the humour in the statement. Korede adjusted himself and tried to collect his thoughts when it suddenly hit him. He blinked repeatedly and frowned at the agent trying to confirm what just came to him. He sat up quickly and bit his finger in thought.

"Sir, is there something you remember?"

Korede ignored the agent as the picture fell in place. After the killer plunged the sword into the pastor, ending his life abruptly, he did something really strange. He removed some pebbles from a pocket in his tunic and quickly stuffed them into the mouth of the dead pastor. But that wasn't what was bothering Korede. In the process of stuffing the stones in the pastor's mouth, Korede had noticed something strange about the killer. The last finger on his left hand was missing.

CHAPTER 19

Thursday 12 September, 2012.

AT ABOUT A FEW MINUTES TO 1 P.M., SIX PEOPLE, hundreds of miles apart discreetly inserted a specially designed ear pod into their ears and waited. They had all received an encrypted e-mail message beforehand with the encryption code sent separately to their personal phones a day later. The message had contained only the day and time of the meeting.

Hussein Alban, veteran industrialist and international businessperson with over two hundred chain of stores nationwide and a prevailing contender for the upcoming governorship election of Yobe State. He was en route to a political party meeting in Damaturu riding at the back of a motorcade.

Majiri Bantaum, media mogul and CEO of Centre Point, the foremost independent broadcasting corporation in Nigeria with international affiliations to the world's leading media organizations in the United Kingdom and the United States. He was seated alone in his private office in Victoria Island.

Sayeed Momodu, a politicized radical having had several scrapes with the SSS on matters of state. He was the most vocal of the lot and wrote regularly for a radical independent publication called *La-zau* in Yemen where rumor has it that he runs an arms dealing cartel. Heir to a fortune from his father, a timber magnate resident in Borno State, he was the perfect eligible bachelor; willing to explore but not commit. He thrived on national controversy. He was alone in a reclining chair by the poolside of one of his many properties in the state.

Zara Achums previously married to an oil magnate from the eastern part of the country but now safely divorced. A professional foreign negotiator who had wriggled the Nigerian government more than once from deals gone awry. She was shrewd, calculative and sexy in that order. Some claimed that if nature were kind enough to offer her balls, they would be football-sized.

Nuhu Mohammed, unassuming, petite and structured. Telecommunication mogul and media charmer with a vast network of links that spanned across the globe. A recent franchise partnership with software giant Microsoft made him the first individual in the world to legally clone the esteemed brand. Secretly, he was a man of peculiar inner stirrings and had a harem of nine wives, the oldest not being more than fifteen.

Aziz Adamu, the Attorney-General of the Federal Republic of Nigeria was comfortably seated in his federally allocated office in Abuja.

Major Haman was merely a commander of men, manager of resources and concocter of conspiracies.

He checked the indicator monitor on the transmitter of his ear pod device to ascertain that all six members were linked, pressed a button to encrypt the frequency signal and electronically fortify it from wavelength eavesdroppers. Next, he requested voice analysis verification from each member and one by one, they uttered the pre-arranged phrase.

The meeting began.

"My friends, I welcome you all. As you are aware, the project has been set in motion and is presently producing the anticipated reaction but we have... eh... a certain unwelcome development that we need to address urgently."

Major Haman paused and listened to the static report coming in, then continued.

"It has come to our notice that one of the contractors is not keeping to the script."

Silence.

"I don't understand it at all, has the contractor completely lost his mind? What is all this business about leaving pebbles on the crime scene, ehn? We need to contain him fast," Majiri Bantaum's husky voice boomed through to the others.

"I totally agree," was Zara Achums quick reply. "He is not only employing unorthodox methods but is taking unnecessary risk. At the last contract, the press had close to 300 eyewitness accounts of the killing and almost a hundred near-accurate descriptions of our man. I don't like it one bit."

There were murmurs of agreement from the other members.

"What do we do about the situation?" someone asked.

"We have to take care of every loose end. He needs to be taken off the project before he becomes a liability," Sayeed Momodu offered.

"Major, can we replace him?" the Attorney-General asked in a half whisper.

"It's not really that easy Sir. The term of the contract was for him to work independently without interference. He made sure of that so we don't have a way of interrupting him once he's been activated.

Silence.

"Then we need to take him out."

"That is correct"

"Do we employ another contractor?" someone remarked bitterly.

"That is the most obvious solution."

Silence.

Major Haman spoke up. "We must remember that we all agreed not to employ a regular for the actual job because of the risk involved. Are we now saying that we are willing to contract another outsider to take him out?"

"I think that would mean allowing more people into the loop which in my opinion is much too risky. We should be tying loose ends not creating new ones," Hussein Alban interjected calmly.

It was the only female member of the A-men committee that finally proffered an answer to the looming challenge.

"We don't want the knowledge of this project to ever get out. Do we?" Zara Achums began rhetorically. Nobody offered a reply.

"Then the answer is quite simple. We contract the two assassins separately to take out each other and since they are already on the SSS hot list, anonymously tip them on details of the survivor. I assure you, knowing how they think the survivor would rather die than be taken alive."

CHAPTER 20

THE SAUDI ARABIAN SPECIAL INVESTIGATIVE POLICE are an offshoot of the General Directorate of Investigation and are commonly called the "Mubahith", which roughly translated means "secret police". They are in charge of domestic security, intelligence collection, analysis, and the coordination of intelligence tasks.

At their National Information Centre in Riyadh is a centralized computer system linking 1,100 terminals that maintain records on citizens' identity numbers and passports, foreigners' residence and work permits, Hajj visas, vehicle registrations, criminal records as well as sensitive inter-agency data.

Agent Goke Davids put a call through to Director General Asaph Omar of the Mubahith and listened to the line go through a series of clicks as the connection was made.

"Good day Sir, this is Agent Goke Davids of the Nigerian State Security Service, we put through an urgent inter-agency request yesterday as regards a lead we are following here. I am calling to check if your agency has anything for us."

Twenty-five minutes later, all the intelligence related to a pebble killing during the last Hajj in Saudi Arabia was freshly faxed to the office of the SSS in Nigeria together with a detailed mug shot of the suspect involved. An independent local maintenance worker from Mecca had been found strangled in his apartment building above his office. The only thing that had been taken were worthless pebbles soon to be delivered to the maintenance office for use in the upcoming Hajj ceremony. A suspect was photographed leaving King Abdulaziz International Airport at Jeddah with the same kind of pebble samples. He was a Nigerian.

The hunch had paid off.

CHAPTER 21

The Presidential Villa, Abuja 7:45 a.m.

LOCATED WITHIN THE THREE ARMS ZONE OF ABUJA Metropolis lies the office and residence of the Nigerian president, unofficially known as "Aso Villa".

The official meeting place in the Presidential Villa is a kaleidoscope of soft brown and cream with a stately Victorian chandelier hanging from the patterned ceiling. Cream cushions arranged in an arc with heavy matching drapes and a hand painted African artifact enclosed in the Nigerian coat of Arms in the centre of the soft brown rug, completed the modest furnishings. The Federal Executive Council of Nigeria had been summoned and was seated when President Bello Gurau sauntered in. In the past month the seemingly larger than life image the President had carefully structured for himself and his administration had been torn apart by the media.

Every member of the Council knew why the emergency meeting had been called.

The whole nation knew.

The Council rose awkwardly but were motioned to remain in their seats by the President as he took his own place in the vacant middle cushion.

"Good morning and thank you for showing up for this impromptu meeting. As you all are aware, we have a situation that is slowly escalating into a global catastrophe," he began in his clipped northern accent.

He studied the faces that peered back at him and continued. "The nation has been held to ransom by an invisible enemy. We have failed to apprehend the enemy within and the press, both local and international, is making news off our misfortune. Please be honest with me, how bad is the situation?"

It was the Minister of Foreign Affairs who spoke first.

"Honestly Mr. President, we have become the laughing stock of the international community and foreign investors are wary of coming in. They are concerned about how secure their investments will be."

"How is our economy faring under all of this bad publicity?" The question was directed to the Minister of Planning and Economic affairs.

The Minister was ready for the question. He pulled out some papers and studied them through his bifocal glasses, cleared his throat and announced in a somber tone.

"The hit we are taking is massive, Mr. President. Several local groups around the country are claiming responsibility for the killings and have put certain communities in constant fear. People have refused to go to work for fear of being targeted. It's a drastic nosedive in revenue acquisition." He adjusted his glasses and consulted his paper again.

"There has also been an escalation of crime in both the urban and rural areas with self proclaimed vigilante groups attacking innocent night marauders in the guise of apprehending the killers. We need the presence of security agents in place to avert a civil unrest."

"I see." President Bello stared straight ahead and sighed.

His gaze finally fell on the Minister of Internal Security.

"Minister Uwaje, how close are you at identifying the people responsible for this… this madness?"

A few council members looked up at the President and then followed the direction he was looking to settle on the Minister. The Minister of Internal Security was the youngest member of the Federal Executive Council and looked every bit his forty years of age. He was a professional in every sense of the word and thoroughly schooled on the intricacies of security matters. With a well groomed afro, a no nonsense deadpan expression and a military antecedent that would make any general look like a boy scout, he had been the obvious and most qualified choice for the much dreaded role of Minister of Internal Security.

"Mr. President, we are still unclear about who is behind the killings…"

A murmur rose amongst the council members.

"…But we have identified one of the assassins,"

The murmur stopped abruptly.

Twelve pairs of eyes were suddenly fixed on Minister Uwaje. It was the President who asked the question that had surfaced in everybody's mind.

"Minister of Security, can you please tell us who this person is?"

"His name is Almadin Umaru."

CHAPTER 22

THE EVENING SALAT WAS ABOUT TO COMMENCE; Almadin squatted before the tap and began the ablution process. With his fingers systematically enmeshed, he washed vigorously. He stared at the missing last finger on his left hand and grinned. It was the result of a childish prank played on him by some bigger Almajiri kids who, out of envy, had abducted him with the intent of scaring him into revealing the location of his daily proceeds. The game had gone out of hand when one crooked kid with badly crossed eyes had actually used a small knife to draw blood from his finger hoping to elicit a faster confession. They finally left him when his screams drew the neighbors. The injury festered over days and the finger had to be cut off to discourage gangrene. Almadin walked into the mosque and in his normal fashion, scanned the room for anything out of place. Satisfied that everything was as it should be, he relaxed and joined in the prayer.

CHAPTER 23

AS A YOUNG MAN, EGUNU HAD FULLY INDULGED. Growing up with a single parent in one of the coastal communities of downtown Lagos had made it easy. He had an unwritten parasitic agreement with his mother. She was to slave to put food on the table and he would do his best to remove it. No contribution on his part was deemed necessary. His only real gift was his ability to "take care" of his own; he was known to be fiercely protective. At 15, he had obtained complete bragging rights on the streets of Ebutte-meta where he lived, leading over a dozen street skirmishes and almost always emerging victorious. Egunu had finally taken up responsibility at home when his mother opened up to him and revealed the circumstances surrounding his birth. Sired by a local auto mechanic in a moment of unbridled passion, he had been vehemently denied and left to his mother to support alone.

The pig!

On his sixteenth birthday, Egunu had quietly sought out his "father" and without any introduction, bashed his head in with a wheel spanner. He had watched him bleed to death on the leather seat of an unrepaired Mercedes Benz.

Pleasure comes only from pain.

In the late 90's, recruitment into the Nigerian Army was considered a fashion statement, so Egunu enlisted. He had learnt early in life that to blend into any setting, you had to acquire a mixture of outward conformity coupled with inner defiance.

The philosophy had helped preserve his sanity during the inhuman military training.

He had learnt quickly in the army, absorbing every detail he came across to feed an inherent crooked disposition that had been unleashed when he watched his father die. In 1987, as part of the ECOWAS mission to Liberia he had joined up with some local mercenaries who had introduced him to a very profitable trade. For the next two years, he had done side jobs for local gangs in the city capital and had prospered secretly. Later he hooked up with a former Russian soldier hiding in Liberia and had been trained professionally on the art of killing.

At the end of his peacekeeping sojourn in Liberia, he bribed an army doctor and was discharged on the grounds of a serious heart condition. He was thirty-one.

When he returned to his community in Ebutte-meta, he discovered that his mother had died of a stroke.

She was always so feeble.

It was now very clear what he would do with the rest of his life. He had been born for it.

CHAPTER 24

"I SUGGEST WE HOLD UP THE ANNOUNCEMENT OF the declaration Mr. President. The news of your wanting a re-election with the present situation in the country would definitely cause uproar."

Azubike Agu, campaign manager for the President's re-election bid was a very practical man. A pound short of being obese with a clean-shaven head and a shock of overgrown beard that made him look like a village chief, he had successfully stirred and implemented the re-election ambitions of two past presidents and was from a slowly diminishing flock of fiercely loyal men.

"I think I agree with Mr. Agu," commented Vice President Patrick Danovo-James

The three men were in a private meeting in the presidential office, the private sanctum of the number one citizen of Nigeria. The walls were done in mahogany wood laced with soft brown finishing. Teal green patterned curtains embellished the east wall and a gallery of photos of past presidents adorned the west. President Bello Gurau sat in his black leather chair with the insignia of the Nigerian Coat of Arms behind him. He had hawk-like piercing eyes that accentuated the worry lines on his forehead, a slightly hooked nose and thin lips that did nothing for his face.

The Vice President continued. "We need to give the people something, make them feel a little secure before they can trust us enough to invest their votes in us again."

Campaign Manager Azubike Agu nodded in agreement, as he watched President Bello's frown deepen. The President placed both palms face down on the huge desk bowing his head slightly and after only a short while, he looked up and spoke.

"Let's call a press conference."

⌘ ⌘

"Fellow Nigerians, for some time now we have watched with unconcealed disgust as some misguided elements have perpetrated an unholy act upon our land by unleashing death upon our citizens. We have watched but that is not all we have done. We have also painstakingly sought the miscreants out. We have seen interest groups and activists take out their frustration on the Nigeria Police Force as a direct result of these killings and we condemn such an act." President Bello Gurau paused and looked up from the speech he was reading. The presidential pressroom was packed full; a cross section of the Nigeria media was fully represented. A few pressmen scribbled nonstop while others held out recording devices with flash bulbs and video cameras, completing the entourage.

"We implore you to cooperate with the government to stamp out this menace. There has been an unsubstantiated rumor that the killings are a brainchild of the Al Qaeda. We strongly refute the allegations. To that effect, we are releasing information about one of the assassins involved in this plot."

The up-till-then silent gathering burst into activity, as twenty media representatives all tried to talk at the same time. The president looked sideways at his official spokesperson who was taking the bench on this one.

He continued, totally ignoring the noisy reception. "Ladies and gentlemen, we have activated all resources to try to locate this assassin in question. His name is Almadin Umaru."

⌘ ⌘

Much later in the quiet of the presidential office, President Gurau stood pacing back and forth while Vice President Patrick Danovo-James watched in amusement.

"I really admire your courage; it was a good move to give the press something to work off their energy."

The President kept pacing and didn't offer a reply.

"I am worried Patrick," he blurted out finally in a half whisper.

"Why are you worried?"

"I want you to run with me Patrick. My re-election campaign is not complete without you. You know that."

The Vice President exhaled, adjusted his native attire self-consciously and smiled faintly.

"Mr. President, you understand that more than anything I want to be by your side again but my health fails me. My heart condition has escalated since the last time and the doctors have advised that I retire from politics to save my life. I am sorry."

The president stopped pacing and stared at the floor.

"I understand, Patrick but..." He managed quietly.

"...I just really need your support."

"Don't worry Mr. President, you will always have my full support, I promise you that."

CHAPTER 25

KOME OGENE IN THE DAYS THAT FOLLOWED pondered endlessly over the simple message that the janitor had scrawled on his bookshelf. *What exactly did it mean? Who in God's name is Manfredi Nicoletti? Or was it a what? Damn! A computer would really come in handy at a time like this.*

The date in the message was the fourteenth of this month, which was in two days.

I can wait.

He had checked for hidden codes in the message but had not seen any. *Maybe it had been cleverly hidden*, he thought. *Maybe.*

God, just five minutes alone with a computer and all this mystery would be successfully unraveled.

He drummed his fingers impatiently on the desktop of his reading table and sighed.

I can wait.

⌘ ⌘

"I want to see the Director."

Kome smiled sheepishly at the burly guard at the entrance of the Administrative Quarters. The guard stared back feigning ignorance.

Imbecile.

"Officer, give me a break here, it's really important that I see the Director. I put in a formal request this morning," he added breathlessly.

The guard grinned, revealing a gap tooth that made him look like a schoolboy.

"The Director's off limit today. State business."

"But it's important that I see him. I need to use a computer for my research."

The guards grin grew wider.

"As important as me getting to marry Agbani Darego, eh?"

Kome hissed and walked away as the guard burst out laughing.

⌘ ⌘

On the evening of the thirteenth, the delivery bag arrived. It was due every fortnight and had to pass thru a 3D scanner check before being sent straight down to the bunker.

A packet of cracker biscuit was delivered to a guard, a carton of cigarette to the Administrative Office and a ventolin inhaler to the Computer Analysis Quarters.

⌘ ⌘

James Kadiri was on duty today. He got up from the bunk and quickly showered. Humming an offbeat tune lightly, he put a comb through his afro as he stared at the full-length mirror. *Mummy was right, I am really a lucky child,* he thought.

A first-class graduate of computer engineering from the university of Zaria, he had been approached while writing his final project by a federal consultant and offered a job with the government. The pay was off the roof but the job required a signed agreement not to ever reveal its details to anyone. Not even to his mother.

James Kadiri started work as a computer analyst with the State Security Service. He had undergone training amongst other first class materials brought in from all over the country.

It was like something from a spy novel.

It consisted of basic training in arms handling, field ops techniques, self-defense and eventually an introduction into the world of information technology. Two years later, he was inducted into a confidential team of professionals to undertake a highly classified project. James began work 20 feet below the Presidential Villa, in the secret facility known simply as "the bunker".

⌘ ⌘

His shift was to start by seven p.m. He finished dressing and picked up his inhaler. It had come with the delivery bag the night before.

Mummy pampers me too much. How did she know that I needed a new inhaler?

⌘ ⌘

Kome paced back and forth in a dizzying trajectory. *Today is the fourteenth, so I ought to know what it all means soon. It's already 6:30 p.m. One more hour to go.*

He strolled past the Administrative Office, the computer analysis section and ended up at the kitchen. *Everything seems to be normal. What the hell is the message for?*

⌘ ⌘

A Slow night. James Kadiri sat with legs crossed on a corner of his desk. The blinking red dots on his computer screen indicated the whereabouts of the twelve inmates or as the Director called them, "state guests". The inmates as long as they remained within the safe zone parameter where allowed to do as they pleased but beyond that point, their dots took on an eerie green glow and set off a high priority alert. The Director was contacted for such an eventuality.

The blinking red dots moved around the facility, crisscrossing like tiny flies in flight.

Restless aren't we? James spoke to no one in particular.

In the bunker, everything was recorded. The behavior of the inmates, their movement patterns, mood infusions, state of mind and a dozen other things were reported daily. Each shift was like a scientific experiment with a whole bunch of data being gathered for later analysis.

James yawned and stretched reaching for his cup of coffee with the same motion. He drank noisily, screwed up his face and dropped in two more cubes of sugar.

Nothing out of character tonight.

He looked up at the air conditioning unit, shuddered and switched it off. *Men, it's really cold tonight.* He peered at the screen again and frowned. *Hmmm. Kome Ogene seems to be extra restless tonight. Something on your mind pal?*

Slowly, still staring at one moving dot on the screen, he imputed the data he was seeing into his report. Reaching out he picked up his inhaler and sucked on it noisily still staring at the monitor.

⌘ ⌘

Kome walked the facility for the umpteenth time trying to maintain an air of casual interest. *Same thing as before. Nothing unusual. The whole thing must have been a practical joke.*

⌘ ⌘

Inside the computer room, James clutched his chest, heaving in pain. He suddenly broke out in a cold sweat and the room temperature felt like it was close to boiling.

What the hell is wrong with me? I can't breathe.

He gasped, looking furtively around the office and making a decision, he headed for the door. There was an overwhelming pressure on his chest that threatened to crush his heart.

I… have t…to get out of the room. The damned heat.

He staggered to the door, managed to type in his security code and as it slid open, his legs gave out from under him and he keeled over and slumped in the corridor.

⌘ ⌘

Kome stopped in his tracks at the sight before him. Lying face down on the marble bunker floor, wedged halfway between the door of the computer room and the corridor was one of the computer analysts. Kome rushed over to the still figure and checked him for a pulse. Nothing.

He's dead!

Then it came to him. This was all part of the message scrawled on his bookshelf. He glanced nervously around and seeing nobody, quickly dragged the dead body back into the room. He stared at the computer before him and his mouth watered.

Manfredi Nicoletti; the final part of the message. I have to find out!

He mumbled something under his breath and sitting down, he began.

It is rumored that an average hacker can find virtually anything in the world in three minutes. That information is not exactly true when the combination included a first class hacker and a super computer. It took considerably less time.

Exactly 1 minute 43 seconds later, Kome knew everything that needed to be known about Manfredi Nicoletti. He was the architect that built the renowned Millennium Park in Abuja and also, known only to a privileged few, the top secret facility under the Presidential Villa known only as "the bunker". A map of the facility appeared on the screen with the various entry and exit points. Kome hurriedly printed a copy.

Bingo!

There was still the business of the chip inserted into every one of the inmates in the facility. If he made a run for it now, they were sure to locate and shut him down when they discovered.

I need Intel on the chip to make a clean getaway.

The microchip was located near the fourth thoracic vertebrae and powered by lithium-uranium amalgam. It would take a steady hand and a medical precision equipment to remove it.

All I need now is time to get to a doctor.

Kome smiled for the first time that day. Time he could create. With a quick drumming of his fingers on the keyboard, he activated a virus he had created a year ago; it was simply called Dark-nest. Taking a last look at the room, he grabbed the dead analyst's security card and fled the scene.

CHAPTER 26

SHE HEARD MOVEMENT ALL AROUND HER AND A FEW inaudible murmurs before the blindfold was finally removed. She blinked to adjust her eyes to the sudden light, a contrast to the darkness of the facial covering.

It looked like an abandoned warehouse.

A voice spoke from somewhere above her, a cultured accent laced with a rich baritone. It had a familiar middle-belt twang to it.

"We are in need of your expertise Miss Linda Ebachie," the voice began.

"..And we have taken extra precautions to make sure you cooperate with us and help advance our interests."

The bastards have my father, she thought.

"Your dear father will come to no harm as long as you do our bidding to the letter. The reverse is the case if you decline."

Linda looked around finally locating the source of the voice on a top floor balcony facing where she was seated. She could barely make out his face because it was shrouded in darkness; a silhouette.

"W...Who the hell are you?" she blurted out finally.

Did he smile?

"I will be your host for as long as you remain in our custody but to my few acquaintances, I am simply known as the Federal Executor."

CHAPTER 27

AGENT GOKE DAVIDS GAPED AT THE TELEVISION screen in shock.

How the hell did they get a lead on the assassin? Details of the suspect Almadin Umaru, had been kept a close secret, so how had the President gotten the information?

He picked up his phone and called his liaison officer in Police Special Branch, Ikeja.

"Inspector Godfrey, did you just hear the President's speech?" Agent Goke queried breathlessly.

"Yes Sir, we are very shocked and don't know how he got the information."

"Don't tell me you don't know how, officer! There is an informant amongst your men, that's how!"

"Eh... Sir, I will find..."

"You will find nothing. I want a list of everybody privy to that information and I mean everybody!" Agent Goke hollered and dropped the phone. *Snitches! Now the assassin will know that we are on his trail.*

By evening that day, the five departmental heads that were privy to the info about the assassin were being tailed and taps had been put on their phones and computers. Agent Goke threw out a smoke screen for good measure; untrue info describing in detail a lead to the capture of the assassin. The suspected departmental heads were all sent a memo.

Okay. Now let's find out who the presidential informant is.

⌘ ⌘

Almadin Umaru had no idea anybody was onto him and even if he did, he would not have cared the least. He never watched TV or any of the new age conveniences that had overtaken the ancient ways. They were a distraction to true worship. A *gurome*; a curse. It was time for the evening Salat and he tried to empty his mind of all thought as he participated in the ablution.

Allah is proud of me. I am a true messenger of the cause of Islam. I have earned the medal of recognition of the Darl-Al-Harb.

He smiled at the other worshippers preparing for Salat alongside him.

Father would be proud of me.

CHAPTER 28

TINY CCTV CAMERAS ARE CONSTANTLY SWEEPING almost every square meter of the new Murtala Muhammed Airport 2 (MMA2) terminal and the footage is relayed to the security office on the second floor, which is manned round the clock by aviation security operatives and men of the Nigeria Police. Today was however different, the security status had been updated to high alert and necessary lethal force had been endorsed. The security operatives on duty had also been discreetly doubled.

Something was happening.

They had gotten an anonymous tip that MMA2 was to be the location of the next religious killings.

All movement within the airport terminal was being monitored, automatically recorded and run through face recognition software that instantly processed the data received in real time. Therefore, it took only about ten minutes for the cameras to spot the suspect, run his face through airport security's recently updated database and get a match. The security operative on duty blinked at the face on the screen, exhaled slowly and picking up the phone dialed a number.

"Sir, we have a match."

⌘ ⌘

The VIP lounge at MMA2 can only be accessed by an executive Gold Card and so is cut off from the rest of the airport. Reverend Beremisi Oron was seated quietly inside with an aide and a poorly disguised bodyguard, sweating in the air-conditioned lounge and waiting for his flight to be called. The aide was filling him in on his itinerary for the coming week but he was not listening.

I can't believe it. I am actually scared.

What person in his right senses would take out a hit on a servant of God? Thirty-three highly respected men of God all over the country were already dead and nobody had as much as claimed responsibility for the senseless killings.

God, what is happening?

His congregation had finally put together some money and requested that he and his family leave the country and lie low until the massacre ended. He had jumped at the idea. His family had already left for the United States the week before and were safely tucked away in Kentucky. For the umpteenth time he stared at the faces of the people seated in the lounge outside and wondered.

What did a killer really look like?

⌘ ⌘

Outside the VIP section in the regular waiting lounge, Kome Ogene sat with a palm top and a small overnight bag at his feet. No one seemed to notice the lone figure as security officials hurried past.

⌘ ⌘

In a small room in the security offices of MMA2, Agent Goke Davids and Edet Mbang of airport security, together with four security officials gathered round the monitors for a briefing. A detailed map of MMA2 was on one computer screen and a frozen camera shot of the suspect entering the terminal from the car park was on another.

"The suspect is most likely armed and dangerous and should not be apprehended alone. I want a two-man team on his tail and on spotting him, backup should be requested immediately!" barked Agent Goke.

Edet Mbang, chief of airport security nodded gravely as he studied the picture. The suspect had a black hat pulled down over his clean-shaven face and was carrying a small suitcase. Edet Mbang quickly radioed the details to the operatives around the airport and uploaded the picture of the suspect to their hand held devices.

There is no way you can escape this one mister, not with thirty security operatives on your tail.

⌘ ⌘

Egunu watched as the Reverend fidgeted. The flight was being delayed due to unfavorable weather and this produced some more fidgeting from the man.

He smiled.

Metaphysicians believe that when a man draws close to his end, by a rare clairvoyant insight he can actually feel death's approach. He grinned at the thought and studied Reverend Oron again.

Feel it, man of God feel it because it will be the last thing that you feel.

⌘ ⌘

Jamiu Akande wasn't supposed to be on duty today. He was standing in for his colleague who had suddenly taken ill that morning and cursed his luck that it was on his watch that a dangerous fugitive had to walk in. He uttered a few choice curses to vent his anger and again scanned the area. As a former police officer, he had been prepped but had not seen much action on the field before he was downsized by the machination of the incumbent government. Work as an airport security operative was more rewarding and entailed little or no violence and so a taser confrontation was as physical as he had ever gotten. He rubbed the sweaty palm that gripped his taser on his shirt front and blinked nervously. Then he saw him. It was definitely him. He produced his hand held device and quickly scrolled to the fugitive detail that had been uploaded to them recently. The man had the same sparse front hairline, thick beard and an ash suit and checkered shirt. There was no doubt. Jamiu quickly flicked on his walkie-talkie and relayed the message and his location to the other operatives around the airport. Slowly without attracting attention, he followed the man who had turned a corner and was heading for the multi storey car park on level two.

⌘ ⌘

Agent Goke listened for a while to the detail coming into his transmitter and frowned. "I want all security operatives to seal the car park. I repeat, seal the car park!" He hollered into the walkie-talkie as he dashed out of the room.

⌘ ⌘

Across the terminal, the announcer from the PA system apologized for the delayed flight and called for passengers waiting to embark to start doing so. Meanwhile security operatives began to converge on the airport car park, guns at the ready.

⌘ ⌘

Kome Ogene packed up his palm top and opening the small overnight bag at his feet, he quickly disconnected the high frequency jamming device inside, slung the bag over his shoulder and walked out of the terminal.

⌘ ⌘

Reverend Oron, on hearing the announcement for his flight jumped up nervously and glancing back at his aide, adjusted his suit self-consciously. The clean-shaven gentleman in a three-piece suit and a hat seated by his side smiled at him and nodded understandably.

"You dropped this sir," Egunu smiled as he handed the Reverend his pen.

⌘ ⌘

At the airport car park, over twenty security operatives with guns drawn and hollering at the top of their voices surrounded the suspect in a 2009 Toyota Camry. He was quickly hustled out, frisked and bundled past staring passengers to the security room.

⌘ ⌘

As Reverend Beremisi Oron walked through the recently installed full body three-dimensional scanner at the check in counter, the machine instantly set off a high-pitched electronic screech that began to build in intensity. The security detail at the counter flinched and clutched both ears as she involuntarily retreated from the source of the deafening sound. Reverend Oron screamed at the sudden pain in his head and covered both ears, as he circled searching for where the sound was coming from.

It was both inside and all over him at the same time. It was like scraping a blunt piece of metal on a freshly tiled floor but about a hundred times louder.

People scuttled away staring helplessly at the hysterical figure of the Reverend. His eyeballs began to swell, straining against tightly attached nerve endings that snaked around it, giving his face a grotesque look. Without warning, he began to dribble spittle and blood from his mouth as the piercing sound grew louder.

Somewhere in the distance, a woman screamed.

Just before Reverend Oron's eardrums exploded into his brain, he remembered the pen that the stranger in the lounge had given him.

God, I am such a fool.

For a brief moment, he had met his killer.

⌘ ⌘

Kome Ogene flagged an *Okada*, the local transport motorcycle, and headed away from MMA2.

Men! It's good to be functioning again.

The job wasn't a big deal but it had left his blood racing. He had been required to jam the signal data of the airport security team and replace a fugitive alert profile with a false photo and data from their own archives sending them after someone else. His employer had called it a test to ascertain whether he still had it in him.

Piece of cake. No biggie.

They had promised him a job that would pit his skills against the first class computer analysts in the country.

First class? I am Kome Ogene. Nobody else is first class.

If they could accomplish the near impossible feat of getting him out of the bunker then they really needed him for something big. That night when he finally stumbled through the complex maze of tunnels that led to a secret entrance out of the bunker, they were waiting for him with a car. It was less than a mile west of the Presidential Villa in a private deserted farmhouse owned by an aging couple.

He burst into laughter startling the motorcycle rider who threw him a glance trying to determine if the passenger he just picked had lost it.

CHAPTER 29

HE WAS IN THE ROOM AGAIN. THE WHISPER OF COOL breeze from a nearby crevice was all he could hear in the near-total silence of the cave. The room was roughly crafted from the mountainside and was empty save for a small woolen centerpiece rug that adorned the uneven floor. Almadin, as still as a statue and as naked as the day he was born, sat cross-legged on the rug with both arms outstretched by his side and his head bowed. His lean muscled body was generously tattooed with Arabic inscriptions and drawings. Every thought was slowly expelled from his system with his soft controlled breathing. A mechanical voice from somewhere in the cave in a continual ancient Arabic mantra, reiterated the simple words that he had heard at least a thousand times. It was an ageless ritual. His ritual.

No enemy of Allah deserved to live.

They speak blasphemy and desecrate the land. They deride the teachings of the holy prophet and make of non-effect the mandate of Islam.

No enemy of Allah deserved to live.

None.

CHAPTER 30

THE PRESIDENT OF THE SENATE OF THE NATIONAL Assembly cleared his throat solemnly and studied the members of congress seated staring at him from the floor. The air was thick with tension. They had just argued through another controversial bill recommendation.

The bill in question had gone through a series of harrowing scrutiny and through the weeks of investigating the bill, some members had employed a poison pill amendment; an undemocratic method to ensure its rejection by the senate. Other opposing committees had attached a rider to amend the bill and ensure its approval through congress.

It was a typical legislative warfare.

It was a Right to Information Bill, where the incumbent government and its various security agencies nationwide would be given the freedom to access and extract information from citizens through the unharnessed use of active surveillance — electronic and otherwise.

Members of the Senate had been hard-pressed to pass this particular bill into law because it alluded to the fact that the government would have the power to spy on any citizen without restraint or a warrant. Members on the floor had argued loud and long over the Right to Information Bill, using the famous filibuster tactic to prolong the debate and delay congress from taking a vote but finally it was time to vote on the Bill.

The President of the Senate adjusted his eyeglasses and glared at the members, catching a few disapproving expressions in the process. The amphitheatre style arrangement of the National Assembly complex with its red leather cushioned seats and near freezing interior fell uncharacteristically silent.

"I move the motion for us to vote on the Right to Information Bill. All who want the Bill to be passed into law, please say aye."

The air burst into a series of baritone ayes that reverberated around the complex.

"All who want the Bill rejected please say nay." He finished in a softer tone.

The reply was deafening.

The Senate President shut his eyes and frowned accordingly. He coughed self-consciously and declared the obvious verdict.

"The nays have it."

⌘ ⌘

The Federal Executor walked into the dimly lit room and squinted, focusing on the man sitting behind the massive steel and glass desk.

"Sir, the Bill did not go through. We did all we could but the members loyal to us were unable to influence it."

Silence.

"Sir, I think we could organize a committee and introduce a mark up to revise the Bill."

Silence.

The man's expression was hard to read with the dimmed lighting of the office space but his shallow breathing was clearly discernible.

"When were you born?"

"Eh.. Sir.. I..." The Federal Executor stuttered.

"I asked a simple question. When were you born?"

"Nineteen seventy two Sir."

"So I am safe to say that you were not around when the Union Jack was lowered and the Nigerian flag hoisted to take its place?"

"Yes, you are Sir." He was recovering fast.

The man stood up from the desk and gazed out the gothic style arch of the office window. The sun setting in the horizon cast a pale yellow glow on his upturned face and revealed a series of worry lines etched on his forehead.

"I was a young man when it happened and I swore to do anything within my power to keep that flag flying high." He finished still staring at the colorful spectacle in the distance.

"It is no news that we are no longer custodians of men of vision in this country. Once upon a time, great statesmen roamed our land. Men who were willing to shed their blood for this nation."

He shook his head back and forth before continuing. "The Right to Information Bill was a lifeline to our government to help effectively monitor militant groups and local terrorists nipping them in the bud before they become a nationwide threat… but not even the President wanted it passed."

He shifted a bit and exhaled audibly. "Murtala Mohammed, Babangida, and Obasanjo, some say, were men who employed extreme measures but they purged this nation of weak leadership; in my opinion a necessary extreme."

"President Gurau is weak… an unacceptable option for true democracy. A wimp. He is undeserving of the mantle he wields." He turned and stared at the Federal Executor who was entranced by the mild outburst. "I have watched from the sidelines how he vetoed the Authorization Bill for military funding last year and muddled the constitution amendment attempts. Now the Right to Information Bill has not survived congress. When will it all end?"

The Federal Executor watched the figure spellbound. An involuntary shudder cut through him. *He really believes in all this.*

When he had been summoned and provided with the details of the plan, the Executor had viewed it as another power thirsty politician strategizing a smear campaign. Nothing he had not seen in the previous administrations that had employed his services. He was a realist and accepted the fact that everybody wanted power but... what was this? A patriot?

"I hope you understand why we are doing all this, young man."

"I do Sir."

The figure finally turned to face the Federal Executor and spoke with poorly concealed urgency. "Then help me... help me rid this nation of this threat."

"I will activate the last phase of Operation A-men, Sir."

"Thank you."

The Federal Executor was dismissed with a wave of the hand. As he left, he heard a muffled sniff. Was the damned politician crying?

CHAPTER 31

EGUNU STARED AT THE PHOTOGRAPH IN THE PACKAGE.

Something is wrong.

This surely is not a pastor. Not with all the tattoos that formed an intricate web around the top half of his lean muscled body. He had been told that all the targets were pastors. Then who the hell was this? *A personal vendetta? A political thug maybe?*

Some of the inscriptions on his body were in Arabic and spanned across his light skinned body mass. His face was grim and determined with sunken brown eyes and prominent cheekbones.

Strange customer. I don't like doing a job with minimum details. Risky.

He had provided the rules and had told Major Haman that under no circumstance were they to contact each other. E-mailed messages of the target together with an account confirmation from his bank were all he required to function. No calls. No face-to-face meetings. That was how he had managed to stay anonymous and untraceable all these years.

A job is a job. I have to do it.

⌘ ⌘

Almadin smiled at the figure in the photograph. *Another infidel.* This one had weak eyes that betrayed his soul but he seemed to have a sturdy structure. He didn't have the benevolent look of a pastor. More like a police officer or a cheap bodyguard.

He quickly memorized the details of the target then lit a match to the enveloped package and watched it burn. He had provided the rules. All the packages were to be hand delivered to a certain Tsangaya school in the area where he later picked them up from the Mallam in charge.

No enemy of Allah deserved to live.
None.

CHAPTER 32

KOME SQUINTED AT THE COMPUTER SCREEN IN FRONT of him.

The fact that he was staring at IBM's latest version of the Blue Gene supercomputer with nearly 300,000 processors connected by a high-speech optical fiber network and a performance speed of nearly three petaflops failed to impress him. He was gone past all that.

Damn! These guys are good.

Their firewall structure was Fort Knox quality. It was constructed using a reverse virus primer. Any crack in its exterior would instantly release a smart virus that immediately scrambled your computer and freeze fried your hard drive.

Good structure, but not too good for Kome Ogene.

He shook his head in amazement. It was much easier to hack the SSS database these days than to access the Federal Government Revenue info.

They had learnt the hard way.

Kome resumed his dialogue of codes.

No computer analyst is good enough to keep me out.

CHAPTER 33

"SIR, WE HAVE BEEN GIVEN THE GO AHEAD TO LAUNCH the last phase of the plan."

Barrister Abdul Aziz, the Attorney-General of the Federation glared at the Federal Executor over thick horn rimmed glasses. He was in his federally allocated office in Maitama district. The office wall space was a gallery of Nigeria's finest law heroes frozen forever in time, beautifully framed.

Barrister Abdul Aziz, though a certified legal practitioner, was not a man given to dialogue. He spoke when speaking was the only option. Fiercely dedicated to himself with a personal motto that "a man that works for himself always dies an employer".

When he had been approached by Major Haman about the Committee, he had immediately seen the possibility of using the plan to achieve a far greater purpose.

The highest post in the land.

A religious scandal of such magnitude with a strategic smear campaign that employed irrefutable proof could result in the sudden impeachment of the President.

A dream he had privately shared with only one other visionary.

Abdul Aziz had grown up a fighter. His father would beat his mum until she screamed for the neighbors to come rescue her. Little Abdul after each episode would withdraw into himself refusing to eat or talk to anybody. A sympathetic neighbor once approached him and tried to comfort him asking him why he was sad.

"I don't have anything against him beating her but it is unfair that he never explains to her why he does it."

⌘ ⌘

He had grown up explaining things to others. People needed to understand why they were being punished. He decided to become a lawyer.

"Do you have both parties required for the operation?"

"I do sir, the hacker is all set to go and the accountant is awaiting our numbers."

"So I assume they are co-operating?"

"The hacker's not a problem, his only motivation is money but the accountant's a bit unstable, she insists on seeing her father every day."

"Handle it."

"Yes sir."

CHAPTER 34

"YOU CAN THREATEN ME ALL YOU LIKE BUT I REFUSE to do any work without my workstation."

Linda Ebachie met the Federal Executor stare for stare.

She's a stubborn one. I need to teach her who's the boss around here.

She continued more softly. "See, I don't know what you are up to and I honestly don't care. All I am saying is that I cannot do any real work without my workstation. It contains the world's best equipment units and besides how do you expect me to move around with this?

The Federal Executor studied the makeshift wheelchair unit Linda was presently on. It was a horrible metal contraption that was as huge as a throne and was mangled on every side with rusted peeling paint.

She's right. The thing is as ugly as a coffin and she looks so fragile inside it. How can this lady be the best accountant in the country?

Aloud he said. "You will have your wheelchair delivered to you."

She sneered and replied. "It's not a wheelchair, it's a workstation."

⌘ ⌘

Work began in earnest at the warehouse. It was a highly sensitive task that could only have been achieved by the best. Highly classified government revenue intelligence was quietly extracted from the most fortified servers in the world and studied by the best accounting mind in the country, then digitally altered and returned in scrambled slots and refreshed in milliseconds to conceal the change from prying electronic eyes.

The Federal Executor watched the duo at work and marveled.

Kome Ogene in a swivel chair facing the twin monitor of the world's fastest computer unit opened up the secure data while Linda Ebachie resplendent in her "workstation" altered them.

If we hadn't tried using other experts to do this same job without success, I would think it was an easy feat.

He grinned as he played a private scenario in his head.

It's a pity we have to kill them.

CHAPTER 35

A WAVE PORTAL IS A STREAM OF CYBERSPACE fragment that given the proper orientation can store enormous amount of data. Fewer than 10 hackers in the world had the ability to create a functional wave portal.

It took Kome Ogene the better part of a week to finish up the spec for the wave portal he was secretly building. He wasn't putting his life in the hands of his abductors without a leverage he could use against them if they decide not to stick to their part of the deal. They had promised to let him go but he wasn't taking chances in case they had a sudden memory lapse.

He had tried unsuccessfully on several occasions to initiate some kind of plan with his fellow lady captive but she wasn't interested.

Women! Even in trouble they were still complex.

The plan was ingenious. The people behind it were obviously thinking overtime. The approach was subtle yet believable and was sure to ruffle a few feathers.

He stole a quick glance at the portal readings on his monitor and adjusted a few parameters then quickly hid the interface behind some documents he was working on. He casually glanced around to check if anyone had seen him.

Nope.

Linda was on her wheelchair workstation scowling at the monitor of the built in computer system and fiddling with the dials.

The bitch doesn't know what these goons are capable of. I have tried to warn her but she is not listening. Well, every man for himself.

CHAPTER 36

THE SMOKESCREEN DID NOT REVEAL ANYTHING.

He had placed tabs on his departmental heads and that too had come up with nothing.

Who else had access to the classified intelligence about the religious killings? Who provided the President with the information that he had made public?

If in truth, the leak did not come from the police department, where the hell did it come from? There is a play here that is unaccounted for and I must get to the bottom of it. If anybody in the world would know who gave the President that intelligence, Dipo Maku would.

Agent Goke tried getting him on the phone and as usual got a busy signal. Dipo Maku was a one-man switchboard. A veteran reporter for the Daily Focus, one of the leading newspapers in the country and one of the few men that was on a first name basis with the President.

The line finally went through and Dipo Maku in his uncharacteristic manner hollered his greetings.

"Hey, Goke my boy, why are you calling me today?"

"Uncle Dipo, I need some info."

"Of course you do. Why else would you be calling? Oya, shoot."

"The name of the assassin that Mr. President released in his press conference.... How did he get it?"

"Is that all? My boy, you disappoint me. I expected something more complex. That creep, the Minister of Internal Security, gave it to him."

"Minister Uwaje?"

"Minister Uwaje."

CHAPTER 37

PRESIDENT GURAU STARED AT THE THREE MOST powerful men in his administration and shuddered but outwardly, he kept a straight face and asked, "What is the meaning of this?"

The Auditor-General of the Federation, closely flanked by the Director of Revenue Acquisition made a formidable team but it was the presence of the controversial Senate President that completed the formidable pair.

"Mr. President that is a question we think you are in a better position to answer."

The Director of Revenue Acquisition quickly produced a suitcase, retrieved some papers from it and passed copies round to everybody. President Gurau slowly collected his copy and scowled at the trio before him.

"I don't understand what this is all about…?"

"Mr. President, please hear us out," interjected the Senate President.

"What you have with you is the quarterly revenue report on governmental contracts allocation for the last six months with a listing of the establishments that got the contracts. Also on the next page is the quotation amount agreed for each of the contracts."

The four men in the room studied the documents closely, although only one of them was seeing it for the first time. The President looked up at the Director of Revenue Acquisition, scowled, opened his mouth to say something but thought better of it.

The Director, unaware of the glare of disapproval he just got, continued. "If you continue further, you will discover that the installment paid out to four of the contractors over time is actually in excess of what was agreed."

President Gurau's scowl deepened considerably. "How did this happen?" he queried quietly.

Nobody answered.

"Eh... Mr. President, that is not all. We investigated the four companies involved and discovered that they are simply a front and without doubt do not exist. We then had an expert follow the money payment trail and came up with some shocking facts." He paused self-consciously and looked up at the Auditor-General for confirmation.

The Auditor-General cleared his throat noisily and spoke up. "The payments we made for those contracts was traced to an off shore clandestine Swiss account. The trail was well hidden through some complex fronts but finally led to the same place. The details of the account and the holder are on the next page of the document in your hand."

Only the President looked down at the document this time while the others stared at him. His face slowly took on a surprising animated transformation.

The Senate President finished gravely. "Mr. President, as you may already have figured out, that account belongs to you."

CHAPTER 38

THE FEDERAL EXECUTOR BIT HIS LIPS AND WENT through the motions of a man deep in thought. He fiddled with a pen and beat his lips again. His eyes moved from Linda to Kome and back to Linda.

"I cannot reiterate how secretive this project is and how discreet you should be about everything you have seen and done here."

Linda scowled and spat out with venom.

"We are not fools mister. We know the stakes involved here and you can be sure that we will keep our mouths shut."

Kome shuddered inwardly but nodded in the affirmative.

He had a nagging feeling that somehow those words would be the reason why they would never get out alive.

⌘ ⌘

Linda Ebachie and her father were dropped in front of their residence. The van made a u-turn and was gone in seconds. Father and daughter glanced around and stared at their apartment. It had been two weeks since they were abducted and they had been treated relatively nicely but a kidnap was still a kidnap.

"We need to call the police, Linda."

Linda nodded but was deep in thought. Something wasn't quite right here. *Why would they let them go and run the risk of their operation being reported? It just didn't make sense.*

Linda's father wheeled her into the living room and went in search of the phone. She scowled and stared at the room suspiciously and tried to locate anything amiss. A clock ticked somewhere in the bedroom. A dog barked outside. A baby screamed from a neighboring house. Something nagged at the corners of her mind but she couldn't place it.

She watched her father as he picked up the phone and entered the kitchen.

Why did they allow them go so freely? Why not keep them hostage until the project was implemented?

It finally came to her just as her father started talking into the phone but it was seconds too late. She understood it clearly. A distant hiss coming from the oven and the hum from the microwave explained it all. Her eyes widened as she made a last effort to warn her father.

The Ebachie residence exploded with a deafening roar spilling dust and debris for half a mile. Experts at the scene later explained that the explosion was due to a gas leak.

⌘ ⌘

Kome dashed and ducked around traffic as he scuttled into the ferry terminal. The goons were still on his tail. They had put him in a van and had requested a place where he wanted to go but he knew there would be no drop off. As the van coursed through traffic, he had casually mentioned the wave portal to his would-be executors. They had freaked out and started making calls while he relaxed and tried to nap. Who wouldn't panic if they found out that their well-kept secret would in a matter of days be in the hands of every newspaper reporter in the country.

They started to threaten him at the back of the van but he wouldn't budge so they knocked him around a bit to get better co-operation. By this time they had reversed and were heading back. When they got to a checkpoint, he started banging on the sides of the van and screaming. The police officers at the checkpoint took notice and a shootout ensued between them and Kome's abductors. Kome escaped in the midst of the gunfire and was gone. Minutes later his abductors were done with the checkpoint distraction and were after Kome again.

Kome bumped into some people in the terminal, apologized and was off again.

A shot rang out as bullets whizzed past his head. He ducked and made for the back door entrance, kicked it open and came face to face with the sea. It was the end of the pier with protective railings separating the platform from a 20-foot drop into the sea. He looked back and saw his pursuers with gun pointed, making their way for him.

I have no choice.

He quickly scrambled up the railings, looked back one more time and then jumped.

⌘ ⌘

The cold seawater hit him hard as he went under. He was a seasoned swimmer so he had no problem pushing his way forward. He surfaced briefly and was met with a rain of bullets from the pier. He quickly gulped some air and ducked underwater again as the bullets zig-zagged around him. Pain shot through his side as a bullet hit him. Blood spurted from the injured side as he swam forward, desperately trying to elude his shooters. His head spun from staying underwater for too long and from his blood loss. The last thing he remembered was a strong current advancing towards him as he mercifully blacked out.

CHAPTER 39

THE PRESS WENT CRAZY, BLEEDING EVERY ANGLE OF the story to ridiculous proportions. The president's dealings with anybody controversial was spun into unimaginable conspiracy theories. The nation was stunned into silence. Then the silence was broken, as group after group in the country started demanding a plausible explanation by the president or his resignation and subsequent prosecution.

The media branded the present administration as a group of common bandits unable to manage the widespread religious killings but quite capable of bleeding the nation's resources in the process.

Nationwide mass student protests began in earnest, demanding the president's immediate step down and the world press caught on. The religious killings quickly took a back seat.

It was the second national fiasco in months.

⌘ ⌘

President Gurau stared at the wall of the presidential office and bit his lips thoughtfully. No line of reasoning made any sense to him. Who would allocate such manpower and reasoning to try to frame him and to what end?

He was a man of few friends and even fewer enemies so who was willing to do this to him. *Who?*

He drummed his fingers on his forehead and frowned accordingly. *God, help me.*

⌘ ⌘

The process of impeaching a serving president of a country was a once in a lifetime feat and a global phenomenon. It was a political warfare of rebuttals and counter rebuttals and could only be initiated when there was irrefutable proof.

This time there was.

President Gurau with Vice President Donovan-James watched quietly as the combined House of Senate and House of Representatives slowly took their seats. They would not be allowed in, so as not to influence the decision making process but could watch the proceedings unseen. They both stared at the 46-inch TV in the President's office as they waited for it all to begin.

It was going to be a messy affair with the whole world at standby waiting to see the results of the three-day sitting.

The Senate President cleared his throat and in his characteristic manner glared at the representatives before him. He went straight to the point.

"Fellow representatives, we have come across proof that point to the fact that our beloved President has been involved in an embezzlement scam of enormous proportion."

The murmurings started softly. He ignored it and continued.

"You all have been sent a brief to that effect. For the next three days we will invite experts and produce documentation as regards the allegation."

He craned his neck and scanned the room dramatically like an aged class teacher and raising his voice he declared.

"Your Job, fellow citizens, is simple enough. You will have to decide if the proof we have presented is enough to impeach President Gurau."

CHAPTER 40

STRONG HANDS PULLED THE HALF DEAD BLEEDING man out of the water and into the boat. He began to cough out a mixture of water and blood as the fishermen without any medical expertise tried their best to save Kome Ogene's life. He gripped one of the men's arm in an involuntary spasm and tried to say something but blacked out with the effort.

The journey back to shore was slow and the fishermen thought they had lost the stranger as they tried to get all the water out of his system but as soon as they hit the shore he stirred and opened his eyes. The local nurse took one look at him and went to work speedily. The bullet had made an entry a few inches above his waistline barely missing his kidney and had exited safely. He had lost a lot of blood and consumed a lot of water and she was skeptical about his chances.

Two days later, he opened his eyes and the next day after that he spoke. He managed to convince the locals that he was shot by armed robbers and left for dead. The tale elicited a tremendous amount of communal sympathy from the locals and Kome was given temporary lodging.

He further convinced the local nurse known simply as Mama Bisi that he would pay for the treatment, feeding and lodging as soon as he was strong enough to walk.

CHAPTER 41

THE REFLECTION OFF THE HUGE DOORS OF THE Silverbird Galleria building was what gave Almadin away. Egunu from the corner of his eyes noticed the man.

Egunu stopped at an ATM point and through the reflection on the screen he spotted the man studying him. Years of surviving on instinct had taught him to spot a stalker from a mile away.

Damn! Why the hell am I being followed?

He took his time and pulled out some cash then trying not to draw attention doubled back to the entrance and chatted with a security guard while he studied the crowd.

How many are they? Who are they? I need to lure them outside.

He stopped at a shop and bought a can beer, pulled out his phone and quickly stepped outside. He veered suddenly to the right and was lost in the crowd.

⌘ ⌘

Almadin hurried outside and stared confused. The man had disappeared. He made for the car park, passing a crowd of people entering the building but couldn't find him.

Where did he go? Did he spot me?

⌘ ⌘

Egunu stood at a corner and regarded the man. He was alone.

That meant he was an assassin and there was a contract on his head. Someone out there wanted him out of the way. He turned around and went to the car park to retrieve his car.

⌘ ⌘

Almadin scanned the car park until he saw the man. He was driving out in a BMW X5 series car with the canned beer still in his hand. As the car passed, the man threw the empty can at Almadin's feet and gave him a military style salute.

CHAPTER 42

SHE HAD TENDED TO HIM AS IF HER LIFE DEPENDED on it.

As he swam in and out of consciousness, it was her face he remembered. Smiling down at him like an angel, bandaging his wounds, and firmly helping him with his drugs.

The blackout would then take over.

She cried when he was in pain and laughed when he was better.

She was an angel sent to him.

My angel.

⌘ ⌘

Bisi never once left Kome's side. There was something about this stranger that fascinated her. She had no idea what he was saying as he mumbled incoherently in his sleep and at other times sat up wide-awake staring at the walls.

She just wanted to protect him from it all.

Her mother, the nurse who had taken Kome in, stared at her several times and grunted her disapproval at her daughter's strange behavior but said nothing.

 Nothing needed to be said.

⌘ ⌘

As he got better, they talked, laughed and touched.

The feeling was crazy but it was mutual. They took long strolls in the neighborhood every evening and watched the lights of barges and canoes as they sailed the smelly waters.

They bonded.

⌘ ⌘

A soft wind started outside interrupting the silence of the night. It swelled with urgency carrying a passion with it that was as fierce as it was demanding. It began to blow a consistent rhythm dictated only by nature. It persisted and persisted, paced and paced. Suddenly, in an earth-shaking climax, the wind exploded into a shuddering tornado and as quickly as it had begun, it was over.

Kome and Bisi lay in each other's arms spent.

CHAPTER 43

KOME GENTLY PUSHED BISI ASIDE AND STARED AT THE TV.

There was a live broadcast of the peaceful protest march by members of the Nigerian Bar Association. Kome watched as the main speaker took the podium and began addressing the crowd.

"…The government does not want to publicly use the term 'domestic terrorism' to describe this national fever but that is the reality on ground. Any nation whose intelligence agency cannot penetrate domestic terrorism, undoubtedly, faces an apparent doom."

He sounds sincere.

"Defenseless Nigerian citizens expect the SSS to infiltrate the killer's underworld activities in order to eradicate the bone-chilling menace they have brought upon the entire…"

Bisi saw the worried expression on Kome's face as he stared at the TV screen and knew that he was struggling with something. He had been like this ever since his recovery.

He will talk about it when he is ready. I have to be patient with him.

"…We will not be a party to partisanship, half truths & innuendos. We demand the truth this time. We deserve to know what the killings are about."

Kome was transfixed to the broadcast, every muscle tense in concentration. It was a large gathering of about five thousand supporters at the Tafawa Balewa Square, only a few paces from where he was.

I have to risk it.

CHAPTER 44

KOME OGENE WALKED BRISKLY PAST THE HUGE horse statues at the Tafawa Balewa Square gate glancing back nervously to see if anyone was following him. The Square was packed full for the Nigerian Bar Association protest rally with a heavy presence of reporters and the media. The legendary Square had huge balcony-style pavilions and horse statues flanking the sides of the entrance resembling twin sentries. The crowd was abuzz and cheered with excitement as speaker after speaker attacked the government's failure in apprehending the perpetrators of the recent killings rocking the nation. The media was strongly represented with mobile transmitting vans parked around the Square because as one reporter from channel 3 television put it, this was arguably the largest gathering anywhere in the nation since the killings started.

Kome quickly collected one of the rally t-shirts being handed out to protesters and donned it hurriedly. He wouldn't put it past his ex-abductors to make an appearance here so it was better to blend in and stay inconspicuous. He fingered the flash drive around his neck consciously and glanced around again. *My leverage.*

Unknown to his abductors he had downloaded the entire schematics of the smear campaign project into a wave portal on the internet and later after escaping, had retrieved it.

How do I get to him without drawing attention to myself?

⌘ ⌘

It had taken close to two years and needless bureaucracy to

finally approve the military budget to acquire the latest XORT 8.0 hand-held facial recognition palmtop. Even then, it was still exclusive to only SSS agents and certain military personnel. The device with only a 3-inch diameter weighed less than a wallet and was the latest in clandestine military weaponry. It had the ability to extract streaming real-time data from traffic cameras, local satellite feed and private CCTV recordings for up to a range of three miles.

The SSS agents detailed to "enforce peace" at the protest rally at the TBS would never have spotted Kome Ogene without the device. A video recording of Kome pushing through the crowd to get to the front of the rally was instantly captured, automatically run through SSS database on the palmtop for facial recognition. In less than ten minutes after getting to the venue, Kome was spotted.

Four ill-disguised SSS agents brandishing palmtops quickly dispersed into the crowd in search of him.

⌘ ⌘

Kome had a distinct feeling he was being followed.

Several people threw him strange looks while a few others hollered and cursed as he pushed through the crowd but the feeling lingered.

A flash of black moved swiftly to his left and he impulsively glanced sideways.

Nothing.

I am scared and it's making me imagine things.

He chuckled to himself and was about to finger the flash drive hanging from his neck again when out of the corner of his eye he spotted him.

The guy's sturdy frame standing out against his well-worn black suit together with military issue sunshades gave him away. An SSS agent at a protest rally was commonplace but one with a palmtop studying every face he came across was a recipe for disaster. They were after someone and he wasn't planning to stay long enough to find out if that person was him.

He picked up his pace, moving with renewed urgency through the crowd.

⌘ ⌘

Two SSS agents spotted him simultaneously. He was the only moving person in the throng. They quickly made a beeline for his position flanking him from both sides while one of them radioed in their position and requested for back up.

⌘ ⌘

Kome saw them looking at him and involuntarily gave a soft yelp as he tried to cut a new path through the crowd. He looked back and immediately ran into a young boy. Out of reflex, he reached out and grabbed the lad stopping him just in time from hitting the floor.

Kome bent over to catch his breath and stared at the boy he was still holding.

The boy smiled and Kome froze.

⌘ ⌘

The SSS Agents stopped. They couldn't find him against the sea of heads and glanced around confused.

Up ahead a few people were looking down at something. The agent signaled his partner for them to check it out.

⌘ ⌘

Kome got up and straightened stiffly.

I have no other choice. Change of plans.

He darted to his left and started heading away from the stage. Suddenly he broke out of the crowd and headed for the polo ground at a run.

⌘ ⌘

They had a visual on him again and picked up pace advancing with caution. The suspect profile had tagged him as an armed and dangerous fugitive. They saw him dash into the polo ground and followed, drawing their weapons.

⌘ ⌘

Kome was trapped. The back gate of the polo ground was locked, together with the other exit points. He dashed into a stall containing public restrooms, entered into one and locked it. Crouching in a corner, he held his breathe and tried to stop shaking.

God, don't let them find me. Please don't let them find me.

⌘ ⌘

The agents burst into the stall and looked round at the restroom cubicles that spanned the entire stall. Using hand signals, they conveyed a silent plan and dispersing into twos began searching each cubicle.

CHAPTER 45

"SIR, THIS IS AGENT BAMIDELE COLE, AREA CODE F6249. We have apprehended fugitive 091. Please advice on protocol to follow."

The Federal Executor blinked furiously and consulted his palm top device for the reference confirmation of the fugitive code. He stared at the report on the screen in shock.

Kome Ogene? That's impossible.

"Fugitive 091 you say? Are you sure about that agent?"

"Yes Sir, I am."

"Agent, have you done facial recognition on the fugitive?"

"Yes Sir, I have a 99% match."

The Federal Executor let out a hysterical laugh hitting his forehead with the palm of his hand repeatedly.

Who says miracles don't happen.

He coughed and cleared his throat loudly.

"Agent how many of your colleagues are with you there?"

"Three others Sir."

"Your location?"

"TBS."

"Agent, is there anything of interest on the fugitive?"

"Negative Sir."

"Your order is to terminate the fugitive and abandon the remains."

"Sir, clarify directive."

"I said terminate the fugitive."

"Yes Sir."

CHAPTER 46

THE BMW X5 COMES WITH A TWIN-ENGINE THRUSTER with a startup time of only 5 seconds with only a deep-throated muffled roar to give it away. Egunu floored the accelerator as he reached Third Mainland Bridge. The 11.8 km length snakelike bridge was empty this time of the night so the car sped past without any obstruction. He checked his side mirror and saw a lone power bike slowly closing the distance between them. He reached into his glove compartment with one hand and retrieved a 9-millimeter Glock pistol, checked to see if it was loaded and cocked it. He glanced at the side mirror again. The bike was only about a 100 yards behind him now.

He stepped on the brakes suddenly and as the tyres screeched to a halt, he turned the car 90 degrees totally blocking the road.

The power bike had no chance. It slammed into the side of the BMW and went airborne, somersaulting over the car to land with a crash behind it.

Egunu scrambled out of the car, gun in hand and stealthily made his way to where the bike had crashed. He ran towards the fallen bike shooting as bullets ricocheted off its metallic surface. He stopped in his tracks and stared at the bike.

The rider was missing. He quickly scanned the area with gun in hand.

Nothing.

Where the hell did he go?

He walked over to the railing of the bridge, gun in hand and looked down. The movement was sudden, silent and swift connecting with his wrist and sending his gun flying into the night. A second well-placed kick sent Egunu staggering back as Almadin vaulted over the railing he had crouched behind to hide.

The two assassins stared, sizing each other up as they circled silently. Almadin towered above Egunu with a well-muscled body and a lithe athletic build but Egunu noticed that he had a slight limp and a bleeding bruise on his left arm from his fall from the bike. Egunu stored the information away to be used in the fight.

Almadin reached down to the area above his left ankle and pulled out from an ankle sheath a wicked looking knife. He circled his wrist with the knife in it as the blade caught the light, smiled and charged. His charge was slow due to the limp so Egunu easily parried the deadly blows. They exchanged blows each trying to get an opening hold on the other as their breath quickened. Egunu threw a short jab at Almadin's ribs followed by a kick at his injured leg but Almadin was expecting the move and quickly sidestepped slashing the other assassin's left upper arm. Blood spurted from the cut arm. Egunu ignored the injury and engaged Almadin again. A series of quick jabs and a roundhouse punch in quick succession sent Almadin staggering backwards. They re-assessed each other with renewed interest, each realizing that he was engaging a professional in close quarter combat.

CHAPTER 47

THE TRAILER SHOULD NEVER HAVE LEFT THE PARK.

The brake was still faulty and was yet to be fixed. The mechanic had promised to come in the morning but Hakeem reasoned that he could make a quick run to Alaba-rago market. After all, it was midnight and the roads would be virtually traffic free.

He pumped the brake furiously to free it from any unseen clog, smiled at his colleague on the passenger side revealing tobacco stained teeth and started the engine. It coughed and jiggled a bit then roared to life. Hakeem reversed and drove the huge trailer with a container load of goods out of the park for the last time.

CHAPTER 48

THE GATHERING AT TAFAWA BALEWA SQUARE WAS disrupted by incessant gunfire. Panic ensued as about 5,000 protesters tried to exit the venue simultaneously. People screamed and fled as the uniformed men tried to calm the stampede. Barrister Korede stared helplessly as he watched his carefully organized rally quickly disintegrate before his eyes.

What the hell was happening? Where were all the gunshots coming from?

He picked up his phone to dial the chief of security for the rally when he felt something tugging at his trousers. He looked down and saw a kid smiling at him.

"Are you lost?" he asked concerned, but the 11-year-old boy shook his head vigorously contorting his face into a frown. He reached into his breast pocket, retrieved a flash disc, and gave it to Barrister Korede.

"What is… who gave you…" he stuttered confused. Femi Adele closed the older man's hand over the flash disc and smiled again.

"The man wants you to have it. It is the answer."

CHAPTER 49

THEY BOTH SCRAMBLED FOR THE PISTOL AT THE SAME time.

It had fallen somewhere in the dark walkway near the edge of the bridge. Egunu reached it first, crouching, he frantically clawed at it and as he got his hands around it, Almadin kicked him hard in the ribs. He sucked in breath sharply as the kick sent him flying hard into the bridge railing. He rolled upright and scrambled quickly to his feet but stopped in his tracks.

Almadin had the gun in both hands pointed directly at him.

Egunu moved like the wind. He quickly side stepped and lunched himself over the railing. Almadin pulled the trigger twice, the shot hitting him in the back as he screamed sailing over the railing into the water 40-feet below.

Almadin smiled and slowly backed away from the edge of the bridge, gun in hand.

⌘ ⌘

Hakeem saw the lone figure at the last moment. He hit the brakes and swerved, the trailer screeched in protest, its huge crane-like head turning at a 90-degree angle and its tyre lifting. Almadin heard it and turned, involuntarily lifting his arm to shield himself as the trailer lost balance and unloaded its entire 20-ton content on him.

CHAPTER 50

BARRISTER KOREDE BIT HIS LIPS, DRAWING BLOOD.

He had called every media house he knew but no one was willing to see his "proof". One media representative even called him a "lying scum". He banged his desk in frustration as he considered the options open to him.

He could go through the regular legal channel but that would take weeks.

President Gurau didn't have that much time.

There was irrefutable proof lying in a flash disc in his computer that the President of the country was being framed yet nobody wanted to listen?

The impeachment proceeding was ending today and once the verdict was passed there was little they could do as regards the proof. It would be regarded as "tendered post-verdict" and would take the courts months to reverse such a priority decision.

Then it hit him. Why didn't he think of it before now?

CHAPTER 51

THEY BOTH STARED AT THE ONGOING PROCEEDINGS as an IT document analysis expert went through the process of authenticating the originality of the documents being tendered. He stressed the near impossibility of hacking the government's revenue info website except through granted access by the incumbent president.

"These are all lies! Lies!" Vice President Donovan-James hollered at the TV screen and walked away to the window.

"Mr. President, how can you bear to watch all this, ehn?" He was red-faced and shook like a man having a fit.

President Gurau just sat quietly, staring intently at the TV. *This is the end of the rope for me.*

CHAPTER 52

"PHONE CALL FOR YOU ON LINE TWO SIR."

Agent Goke gently placed his pipe on the ashtray, frowned and picked up the phone.

As he listened, his frown deepened. He started to get up then sat down again.

A dozen questions came to his mind but he asked only one.

"Where are you now?"

Agent Goke dropped the phone, grabbed his keys and dashed out of the office.

He forgot to carry his pipe.

⌘ ⌘

About two hours later Agent Goke accompanied by veteran reporter Dipo Maku stared at Barrister Korede's alleged proof.

Dipo Maku smiled inwardly. *It was a reporter's dream. Classic, conclusive and controversial! The scoop of the year that would create a mountain of a scandal.*

Agent Goke scratched his head thoughtfully. *God! This was dangerous stuff. Some people must really want President Gurau out of the way.*

Korede glanced from one man to the other. They were both lost in thought.

He asked, "What can we do about this?"

CHAPTER 53

THE LAST PHASE OF OPERATION A-MEN WAS NEVER formerly discussed because there was never a last phase.

The Attorney-General of the Federation was the only other person that knew what it was.

It was his plan.

Months ago when Operation A-men had been presented to him by Major Haman, he had immediately known that there had to be a way to tie up loose ends.

A necessary evil.

If you put together a group of the most shrewd and intelligent minds in the country on a project, then you definitely needed a fall back plan to keep them in check in case the project went bottoms up.

Abdul Aziz picked up his phone and called Major Haman.

⌘ ⌘

Radioactive phosphate when properly cultured has a negligible emission rate but even the most precise engineering cannot completely stop a radioactive element from emitting its content after a while.

Each of the specialized ear-pods handed to every member of Operation A-men was programmed to leak its deadly radioactive content after a specified period.

The catch was that no one was told about it.

So depending on the level of proximity to the device, each

holder absorbs a small quantity of radioactive phosphate per time into the body until the body breaks down completely.

Radioactive phosphate was chosen for its unique ability to disappear without a trace in the human body after only a few hours.

Major Haman finished listening, dropped the phone and nodded slowly. He had been given the go ahead to activate the final phase of Operation A-men.

Clean all traces.

On cue, he activated the ear-pods.

CHAPTER 54

DIPO MAKU WAS NOT CALLED A VETERAN REPORTER for no reason.

He had sent a national emergency broadcast message strictly reserved for war alerts and military coups. All major TV and radio stations had been advised to hook up for a high alert message from the presidency.

He smiled at Korede as he edited the footage with a short documentary.

"We need to add some drama to the information so it sticks." He adjusted the camera and began recording his narrative of the ordeal.

⌘ ⌘

Agent Goke wasn't going to be available for the live broadcast; he had procured a small secretive task force and was on his way to the National Assembly to stall the ongoing impeachment proceedings.

An official report would take too long. The proceeding was without doubt illegal. As the police truck sped towards the National Assembly venue, he wasn't sure how he was going to convince anyone about the proof he had just seen.

He was hoping that Dipo Maku would come through with the broadcast as promised.

It was going to be a disaster.

CHAPTER 55

THE ATTORNEY-GENERAL'S FACE DRAINED OF COLOUR as he listened to Dipo Maku on the phone. He was saying something about having proof that President Gurau was innocent.

What was the fool talking about?

"We are broadcasting immediately on national TV so the proceedings can be stopped." Dipo Maku smiled to himself. "Brilliant isn't it?"

"Eh... Dipo, don't you think I should see the evidence first? We need to ascertain whether this proof has anything to it or if it's just a hoax.

"A hoax? Abdul my man, you seem to forget that I was once a legal practitioner."

He laughed some more as he recalled their experiences in law school. They were course mates back in the day.

Abdul Aziz laughed nervously as he wracked his brain for an explanation. What information did he have in his possession and where did he get it from? Knowing Dipo Maku well, he was never one to peddle false evidence. He usually researched everything with a fine comb.

The only way to find out was to see the evidence.

"When are you going on air?" he finally asked after a long pause.

"In ten minutes my man, in ten minutes. So just sit back and switch on your TV Mr. Attorney General and enjoy the show sir." He burst out laughing.

Abdul Aziz drummed his fingers on the table and waited.
"Where are you broadcasting from?"
Dipo stared at the phone surprised.
Strange. Why was he asking that?
"Hello? Dipo, did you hear me? I asked where you are broadcasting from."
"Daily Times, Ikeja."

CHAPTER 56

THE SECURITY OFFICIALS AT THE NATIONAL ASSEMBLY were grim faced and unyielding. Agent Goke was told to stand down and an argument ensued.

It was unclear who started it first but after the soldier in charge called in to report Agent Goke's claim he returned stone-faced but with a worry line now etched on his sun-blackened face.

He looked around at his men and then at Agent Goke's men.

"Oga, you need to go now unless we go open fire."

Agent Goke blinked in disbelief. He couldn't believe what he had just heard.

"Are you mad corporal? You want to open fire on us?"

As if on cue, the soldiers cocked their guns and pointed them at agent Goke and his men.

They stepped back involuntarily and lifted their own weapons.

Somebody opened fire and all hell broke loose.

⌘ ⌘

A priority alert was received at the army barracks at Ikeja and six half-drunken soldiers were scrambled to *Daily Times* office, Ikeja. Their mission was to stop an attempt to broadcast a propaganda message over major networks in the country.

A coup attempt.

Their directive was simple.

Kill everyone in the broadcast room and destroy everything in it.

⌘ ⌘

"We are going live in 60 seconds everyone. Stand by please!"

Dipo Maku adjusted his shirt as make up was applied to his face.

"Counting down now!" the production assistant hollered nearby.

Dipo Maku smiled at Korede who sat near him fidgeting. Dipo was a natural, enjoying all the attention.

A loud bang on the door startled everyone.

The production assistant frowned as he approached the door holding up his hand to temporarily stall the production.

⌘ ⌘

The soldiers with a well-placed kick brought down the door and found the broadcast room empty.

They stared confused at the empty room. A few of them hissed in anger, they had hoped for a shoot out and were obviously disappointed.

They paraded around the room kicking at useless files strewn all over the place and some outdated broadcast equipment.

Their senior officer quickly made a call. "*Oga*, the room is empty. Nobody is here."

They were directed to move out and remove every evidence that they had ever been there.

They left as quickly.

⌘ ⌘

The person at the door had some breaking news to deliver. There had been a shoot out between some soldiers and SSS agents at the gate of the National Assembly, venue of the impeachment proceedings; eight officers were lying dead, and two badly wounded.

Agent Goke had caught two bullets in his left arm, inches away from his heart and was in the hospital.

Dipo Maku nodded gravely as he took in the news. It was now all clear to him.

The broadcast began.

CHAPTER 57

ABDUL AZIZ FINALLY MADE THE CALL HE MOST dreaded.

He was to handle all emergencies and only call the number as a last resort.

It was the last resort.

⌘ ⌘

His phone began to buzz.

He stared at it and scowled. Developing a sudden fit of coughing, Vice President Danovo-James excused himself and left President Gurau's office.

⌘ ⌘

"Sir, they have proof of everything. We tried to stop them but they are broadcasting it live on national TV as I speak to you." Vice President Danovo-James deflated visibly and the phone began to shake in his hand.

"H... How bad is it Abdul? The truth?"

"Sir, it must be bad because Dipo Maku is involved."

He switched off his phone, entered his own office and put on the TV. The broadcast took less than an hour but fifteen minutes would have done just as good.

He shook his head all through it and mumbled to himself.

He calmly reached into his desk, stared at a framed picture

of his daughter on his table, picked up the pistol and shot himself in the head.

CHAPTER 58

THERE WAS NEVER ANY OFFICIAL INVESTIGATION.

As expected, a Committee was set up to look into the attempt to frame President Gurau.

The Committee was liberally paraded on national TV to appease the relentless press and was instructed to give reports at specified intervals.

The reports were never officially released.

A vague description of the Committee's findings were offered instead.

Over time the public outcry over the framing of President Gurau fizzled out and the religious killings miraculously stopped.

No one ever made a connection between both incidence.

⌘ ⌘

President Gurau unleashed the forces at his disposal with a vengeance.

The Attorney-General was apprehended and in typical lawyer fashion agreed to cut a deal to save his neck and lighten his sentence.

He sang like a bird.

A nationwide alert was issued for the arrest of one Major Haman who had fled the country.

In a strange and seemingly unrelated occurrence, eight priority citizens in the country died mysteriously over a three-week period. A national mourning was called for.

The Federal Executor was arrested and jailed, together with eighteen SSS officials for participating in various capacities. Their statement was that they were functioning under the directive of a superior officer on a high alert assignment straight from the Office of the President.

Vice President Danovo-James was given a presidential burial, complete with a full parade and a twenty-one hero's gunshot salute.

The explanation for his death was that he had buckled under intense pressure from the frame-up attempt of his good friend President Gurau.

www.ingramcontent.com/pod-product-compliance
Lightning Source LLC
Chambersburg PA
CBHW021200110726
47900CB00002B/667